The Smallest Girl Ever

written and illustrated by
Sally Gardner

 DIAL BOOKS FOR YOUNG READERS

DIAL BOOKS FOR YOUNG READERS
A division of Penguin Young Readers Group • Published by The Penguin Group
Penguin Group (USA) Inc., 375 Hudson Street, New York, NY 10014, U.S.A. • Penguin
Group (Canada), 90 Eglinton Avenue East, Suite 700, Toronto, Ontario, Canada M4P 2Y3
(a division of Pearson Penguin Canada Inc.) • Penguin Books Ltd, 80 Strand, London
WC2R 0RL, England • Penguin Ireland, 25 St. Stephen's Green, Dublin 2, Ireland (a division
of Penguin Books Ltd) • Penguin Group (Australia), 250 Camberwell Road, Camberwell,
Victoria 3124, Australia (a division of Pearson Australia Group Pty Ltd) • Penguin Books
India Pvt Ltd, 11 Community Centre, Panchsheel Park, New Delhi - 110 017, India • Penguin
Group (NZ), Cnr Airborne and Rosedale Roads, Albany, Auckland 1310, New Zealand
(a division of Pearson New Zealand Ltd) • Penguin Books (South Africa) (Pty) Ltd, 24
Sturdee Avenue, Rosebank, Johannesburg 2196, South Africa • Penguin Books Ltd,
Registered Offices: 80 Strand, London WC2R 0RL, England

The Smallest Girl Ever / The Boy Who Could Fly • First published in the United States
2008 by Dial Books for Young Readers

The Smallest Girl Ever • Published in Great Britain in 2000 by Dolphin Paperbacks
An imprint of Orion Children's Books • A division of the Orion Publishing Group Ltd
5 Upper Saint Martin's Lane, London WC2H 9EA, England • Copyright © 2000 by Sally
Gardner

The Boy Who Could Fly • Published in Great Britain in 2001 by Dolphin Paperbacks
An imprint of Orion Children's Books • A division of the Orion Publishing Group Ltd
5 Upper Saint Martin's Lane, London WC2H 9EA, England • Copyright © 2001 by Sally
Gardner

Printed in the U.S.A.
10 9 8 7 6 5 4 3 2 1

Library of Congress Cataloging-in-Publication Data
Gardner, Sally.
[Smallest girl ever]
Magical kids : The smallest girl ever ; The boy who could fly / written and illustrated
by Sally Gardner.
p. cm.
The smallest girl ever was published in 2000 and The boy who could fly was published
in 2001 in Great Britain by Dolphin Paperbacks.
Summary: Two stories about children who, after enduring difficulties in life, develop
magical powers that improve their lives immeasurably.
ISBN 978-0-8037-3159-2
[1. Magic—Fiction.] I. Gardner, Sally. Boy who could fly. II. Title.
PZ7.G179335Maf 2008
[Fic]—dc22
2007011648

★

To a life sadly ended: Joan Gardner

And a life just begun: Ruby O'Kane

★

The Smallest
Girl Ever

1

Mr. and Mrs. Genie wanted a baby.

They had always gotten what they wanted, so they were sure they would have a son. He would grow up to be a great genie like his father and a great magician like his mother. Mr. Genie was the latest in a long line of genies dating back to the earliest fairy tales, and his beautiful wife Myrtle won the Young Magician of the Year competition when she was only five. Magic ran in the family.

There was only one snag. Mr. and Mrs. Genie had a little girl.

"A girl!" wailed Myrtle. "I wanted a son and heir! There must be some terrible mistake."

"This is too much!" said Mr. Genie. "Never in all my life have I failed to make a wish come true!"

Myrtle sobbed miserably.

"Never mind, my darling," said Mr. Genie, trying to be cheerful. "We can always have a boy next time."

Mr. and Mrs. Genie did their best to get over the shock. It was very hard. They started making plans. They finally called the baby Ruby, and put her name down for Wizodean Academy. This was one of the world's top schools for magic, and it prided itself on only taking exceptional boys and girls.

But by the time Ruby was six, she had shown no sign of any early magical talent. Neither did she have a baby brother.

"Where did we go wrong?" cried Myrtle. "We still haven't got the son we wanted and planned for. All we have is a daughter with no magical talent. It hardly seems worth all the effort and inconvenience of having a baby."

Things might have gone better if Ruby had been a great beauty like her mother. Sad to say, she was a rather plain-looking girl. In short, Ruby was a huge disappointment.

Mr. Genie and Mrs. Genie were far too big stars to be bothered with a child who showed no magical talent. They were at the height of their fame. They threw huge parties, were featured in all the papers, wore expensive clothes, owned the Ferrari of flying carpets, and never gave money a thought. Why should they? They were, after all, entertaining the rich and famous and were in huge demand all over the world.

So Ruby stayed at home with a dull but kind nanny, kept well away from the razzmatazz that made up her parents' life.

Nanny didn't believe in magic. She believed
in the three Rs: reading, routine, and rules. This
way Ruby Genie, more forgotten by her parents than thought about, managed to reach the
grand age of nine without once having gone
to school. Ruby would have liked to go to the
local school with the other boys and girls her
own age, but this was out of the question. Since
she had failed to pass the entrance exam for
Wizodean Academy, her parents had lost all

interest in her education. Which was a pity, for Nanny had taught her to read well and she was quick to learn.

But reading and writing meant nothing to Mr. and Mrs. Genie. A child who could do magic shouldn't need to bother with all that. Ruby might be able to read *Cinderella,* but it would be far better if she could turn pumpkins into carriages.

"You'll just have to work harder at your magic," said her mother.

"I'm sure you're just not concentrating enough on your spells," said her father.

"Oh dear," said Nanny. "No good will come of all this magical nonsense."

And Nanny was right.

2

Just before Ruby's tenth birthday, the emperor of Tishshan, a small and much overlooked state on the borders of China, invited Mr. and Mrs. Genie to perform a magical feat that hadn't been attempted since the pyramids were built. This was far too tempting a challenge. Sad to say, it also proved to be the death of Mr. and Mrs. Genie, who disappeared in a spectacular meteor of fireworks. All that was left behind was a lamp, a wand, and a pile of unpaid bills.

To lose one parent is a terrible misfortune. To lose two is just plain silly, and tends to turn the future upside down. At the tender age of ten, Ruby was an orphan.

The bad news brought with it a lawyer, who appeared like a rabbit pulled from a top hat.

"A very sad business. Such great stars! I remember seeing them perform live at the Met in New York. Quite wonderful! Unfortunately, not so wonderful with money. In short, and not to put too fine a point on it, the house will have to be sold."

"But what about Ruby?" asked Nanny. "What's going to happen to her?"

"Ruby," said the lawyer, searching his papers. "It says nothing about jewelry. Any jewelry will of course have to be sold."

"No, no!" said Nanny crossly. "Their little girl, Ruby."

The lawyer looked quite surprised to find there was a little girl in the room. He pulled even more papers out of his briefcase.

"Here, I have it." He cleared his throat and read, "In case of any unforeseen misfortune like death, having no other living relatives, Ruby, the only child of the late Mr. and Mrs. Genie, is to go to a boarding school for magic."

"But that's ridiculous!" said Nanny. "The girl can't do any magic."

"That," said the lawyer, "is not my problem."

Finding a school of magic that would take Ruby was difficult. She tried once more to get into Wizodean Academy. Not surprisingly, she failed. The school refused to take a child with no magical talent, even if she was the daughter of Mr. and Mrs. Genie, and they felt it was a great mistake that she had been allowed to learn reading and writing.

Ruby also failed to get a place at several other well-known schools for magic, for the same reasons.

"If only they had wanted you to go to a normal school instead of all this magical nonsense," said Nanny, as yet another refusal letter landed on the doormat.

The house was being packed up around Ruby and still no school had been found. The lawyer was becoming concerned.

"There are always orphanages," he said gravely.

Then out of the blue, just before the moving van arrived, came a letter from Grimlocks School for Conjurers and Magicians. To everyone's amazement, Ruby was being offered a scholarship. The lawyer accepted the place immediately without putting himself through the inconvenience of looking at the school.

No time was wasted in packing Ruby up. All she owned in the world went into her suitcase: her new school uniform, her mom's wand, and her dad's lamp. These she had been given by the lawyer, who thought, wrongly, that they had little value except to Ruby.

Nanny said a tearful good-bye. She was sad to be leaving Ruby, but delighted to be taking a job with no magic in it whatsoever. She was going to look after a little baby boy whose parents were librarians.

"Look after yourself, and remember the three Rs," she said. A SOLD sign went up outside Ruby's house. The lawyer snapped shut his briefcase, shook Ruby's hand, and was gone, as was everything else that had made up Ruby's life.

3

"Grimlocks School? Never heard of it," said the taxi driver. Ruby showed him the address again. They had been driving around in circles. Ruby was sure they were completely lost when they came across a battered sign covered with ivy.

As they drove up the driveway, Ruby's heart began to sink. The mock Tudor building, half hidden in a dark wood, was a gloomy sight.

"Not a very cheerful-looking place," said the taxi driver, helping Ruby out with her suitcase. "Are you sure you're going to be all right?"

At that moment the front door opened and the headmistress, Miss Pinkerton, came out. She was a large lady shaped like a bell.

"Ruby Genie? We have been waiting for you," she said briskly. "This way, if you please."

"Good luck," said the taxi driver.

Ruby was shown into the headmistress's office. The room was full of noisy ticking clocks of various shapes and sizes.

"A little hobby of mine," said Miss Pinkerton. "Well, sit down."

Ruby sat, or rather perched, on the edge of a huge chair.

"I must say how pleased we are to welcome you to Grimlocks. We are not a big school, but our aim is to turn out boys and girls who are a credit to the world of magic. You are the first child ever to be given a scholarship by us. We feel sure that with such brilliant parents, you are bound to be a very gifted little girl. Now, I will tell you what we expect from our star student."

Ruby was never to find out what was expected of her, for at that moment, all the clocks started to chime one after another. It was a whole five minutes before she could hear one word of what the headmistress was saying. Then Miss Pinkerton stood up.

"Glad we sorted all that out," she said.

Ruby felt the moment had passed to say anything about not having magical talent. Meanwhile, Miss Pinkerton had not moved. She kept looking at Ruby as if waiting for something.

"Haven't you got something for me, Ruby?" she said at last.

Ruby looked baffled.

"The lamp, your father's lamp!" said Miss Pinkerton. Ruby opened up her small suitcase and took out the lamp. The headmistress seized it and held it up to her ample bosom.

"To hold such a lamp as this!" she cried in tones of delight, before locking it up in a glass display case.

"But I would rather like to keep it with me, if it's all the same to you," said Ruby. "It's all I have to remember my father by."

This was not the right thing to say. Miss Pinkerton seemed to puff herself up like a toad.

"Keep it?" she said, going very red in the face.

"A lamp of this magnitude in the hands of a child! You must be out of your mind. Did I see a wand in your suitcase too? Give it to me, please."

The wand was put in her desk along with peashooters, stink bombs, catapults, and all the other things the children were not allowed.

After Ruby had unpacked, she was taken into the dining hall. A smell of stale cabbage greeted her. About fifty children were seated on benches at two long wooden tables.

"This is our scholarship pupil, Ruby Genie," said Miss Pinkerton.

Ruby took her place at the table between a boy called Zack and a girl called Lily whose hair was in braids.

"You couldn't turn this into chips and sausages with lots of tomato sauce, could you?" said Zack hopefully.

"No," said Ruby sadly, looking down at the pale gray lumpy things that made up supper.

"It must be wonderful to be as good at magic as you," Lily said.

Ruby smiled weakly. She wished more than anything that she was any good at all.

4

The next day, in the school assembly, Miss Pinkerton was in a good mood. It had been a stroke of brilliance, she thought, to offer Ruby a scholarship. It couldn't be a better advertisement for Grimlocks and was bound to bring in other children whose parents had money that was much needed. It would also keep the Grand Wizard happy. Last year, he had nearly closed the school down due to its bad teaching and dilapidated buildings.

"Now, children," said Miss Pinkerton, giving a rare and terrible smile. "You have by now all met our star pupil, Ruby. Ruby dear, will you come up here."

Ruby walked up onto the stage at the end of the hall, where the staff and headmistress were seated.

"I'd like to introduce you to our staff. Miss Fisher, magimatics; Mr. Gaspard, conjuring tricks; Madame Vanish, grand illusions; and lastly myself, special effects. Now Ruby, I am sure you can't wait to show us your magical skills, so I thought you could start by doing something simple, like a little flying or perhaps a disappearing act."

Ruby felt her knees begin to shake. She stood in front of the whole school, hoping that the floor would open and swallow her up. There was a moment of dreadful silence as she stood frozen to the spot. Everyone was looking at her.

"Whenever you are ready," said Miss Pinkerton impatiently.

Ruby felt herself getting smaller, a very strange sensation. Suddenly she had a brainwave.

"I'm awfully sorry, but I only ever did magic with my mom and dad. I'm not used to having so many people watching."

Miss Pinkerton looked much relieved at this explanation and said in a very solemn voice to the whole school, "Ruby has suffered the dreadful loss of her parents, the great Mr. Genie and his wife Myrtle. We must give her time to settle down, but I'm sure in due course Ruby will amaze us with her magical ability and no doubt be able to teach all of us a thing or two."

Ruby wasn't sure about that. All she knew was that she felt smaller.

"That's pretty cool," whispered Zack as she took her seat.

"What is?" said Ruby nervously.

"The way you shrank just now."

What on earth was happening? Ruby had no idea.

If this was what school was about, it must all be a dreadful mistake. How could any kind or loving parent send their child here? As far as Ruby could see, all the parents who had children at the school thought they were doing the very best for them. Zack's mom worked overtime in the circus so that she could pay the school fees. Lily's dad and mom hadn't been on vacation for years so that they could afford to send her to Grimlocks. This seemed true for most of the pupils.

It soon became clear to Ruby that none of the teachers knew all that much about magic. She remembered her father saying in an interview for a Sunday paper that magic couldn't be taught. It came from the heart. You either had it or you didn't. Ruby knew she didn't.

Ruby couldn't make heads or tails of the lessons in magic. Madame Vanish's classes seemed to be in another language altogether. Ruby could hardly understand one word of what she was saying, so there was no hope of her learning anything about illusions. Miss Pinkerton's classes were the dullest, and went on forever. They had little or nothing to do with special effects, but a great deal to do with money, or rather the lack of it. Miss Pinkerton constantly reminded them how expensive it was to run a school like Grimlocks and how she needed to raise more money for a spells lab.

Mr. Gaspard's conjuring classes were the best. Everyone enjoyed them. In his youth he had starred at the Lyceum Theater, but it burned down in mysterious circumstances. What these were he wouldn't say, but a lot of his conjuring involved smoke and most of his lessons ended in a loud bang. He was kind to Ruby and seemed to understand that she was doing her best.

What saved Ruby and made her more friends than any amount of magic was reading. No other child in the school could read. Reading, writing, and arithmetic were not on the school curriculum. The theory was that truly magical children didn't need to be taught these harmful subjects. Reading gave children the wrong ideas.

Ruby's success lay in her old fairy tale book, which she read to her friends after lights out at night. All her friends agreed that reading was quite an amazing magic trick and they all wanted to be able to do it. Mr. Gaspard would let Ruby off having to do any magic, as long as she read aloud to the class. So Ruby managed to get out of having to do anything spectacular—but it couldn't last. Miss Fisher, who taught magimatics, did not like it one little bit when she found that Ruby could read, and she told Miss Pinkerton so.

"What we need," said Miss Fisher, "is a scholarship student who excels in magimatics, not reading."

Miss Pinkerton agreed. "Her father, you know, was an exceptionally clever genie. Perhaps he felt it was all right for her to read."

Miss Fisher sniffed. "So far she has shown no ability at all in the field of magic."

"I'm sure," said Miss Pinkerton, "that when she has settled down, we will find that we made an excellent choice in giving her a scholarship."

"Well, I hope you're right, Headmistress, be-cause I don't think it will go down well with the Grand Wizard if he finds out that we have given our one and only scholarship to a dud."

6

It was the time of year when the Grand Wizard made his annual visit, and Miss Pinkerton was in a panic. She knew he would not hesitate to close the school down if things hadn't improved.

On the whole, there was very little magic attached to getting the school ready for inspection. It was more like a lot of hard work. It was generally agreed that rain would be a bad idea, so a shabby old marquee was put up in the grounds and Madame Vanish did a magic spell to keep the rain away (well, that was what everyone thought she was doing).

Mr. Gaspard was hard at work in the kitchen, trying to conjure up a magnificent tea. Lily was helping him. After a lot of explosions with flour, Miss Pinkerton said it would be better to order some cakes from the bakery.

As for Ruby, she was sitting alone in an empty classroom, wondering what she was going to do.

Miss Pinkerton had given her a list of tricks she was expected to perform for the Grand Wizard, and she was excused from all the classes so she could practice. But it was no good. She still hadn't done one thing to merit a place, let alone a scholarship, at Grimlocks.

Her friends Lily and Zack tried their best to help her. Lily wondered if she could make a smokescreen to distract the Grand Wizard, since she was one of Mr. Gaspard's star pupils. Zack felt the best thing she could do would be to disappear for the day, but this didn't look possible, not with Miss Pinkerton's beady eye on her.

In the end, Lily said, "You could try reading him a story. Perhaps he can't read either."

7

Finally the day of the visit arrived, and it rained. The children were all neatly turned out and if you half shut your eyes, the school looked passable. Miss Pinkerton had made a great show the night before of making the final special effect. Everyone had clapped, though no difference could be seen whatsoever.

The Grand Wizard was a tall man with a long beard that trailed on the floor. He didn't seem much impressed with anything Grimlocks School had to offer. He watched despairingly as one of the juniors did a piece of magic involving fire and smoke that nearly set the marquee alight. He sat, grim-faced, as a senior did a mysterious disappearing act and failed to reappear. Lunch did not make things any better. The sandwiches were soggy from the rain and the water that had been used to put out the fire. And for some reason, the cook had gone missing, as had all the cakes that Miss Pinkerton had ordered at vast expense from the local bakery.

In short, the Grand Wizard was not in a good mood.

"We have of course our scholarship student," said Miss Pinkerton desperately. "I'm sure, Grand Wizard, you would like to see some of her truly amazing magic."

"It would make a change, Miss Pinkerton, to see anything magical at this school," replied the Grand Wizard.

"Ruby, come here, my dear," called Miss Pinkerton. "Grand Wizard, this is Ruby. Her parents—"

"Yes, yes," said the Grand Wizard. "Do you think that we could get to the magic? I do have a dinner appointment at Wizodean Academy that I would like to keep."

This was the moment that Ruby had been dreading. She had been practicing a little magic show that involved pulling a rabbit from a hat, followed by three doves. The rabbit and doves were under the table in two separate baskets. The trouble was she hadn't mastered how to get the rabbit and the doves from the baskets into the hat. She could do it if no one was looking. But *everybody* was looking and Miss Pinkerton, in particular, was looking furious. Mr. Gaspard was looking worried, Madame Vanish was looking bored, and Miss Fisher was looking smug.

At that moment, Ruby knocked over the baskets. The rabbit hopped out from under the table and started nibbling the Grand Wizard's beard as the doves flew away into the rafters.

Once again, Ruby felt herself shrinking with fear, getting smaller by the second. Nothing to do but tell the truth, she thought.

"I can't do magic! It's all been a terrible mistake. I can read, and I can write, but I can't do magic. My parents could, but I can't." At that moment, a dove's poo plopped onto the Grand Wizard's shoulder.

The Grand Wizard stared hard at Ruby and turned pale.

"What is the name of this girl?" he asked, pointing at her.

"Ruby Genie," said Miss Pinkerton apologetically. "Don't worry, Grand Wizard, she's in good hands."

8

It had gone worse than even Ruby had thought possible. The Grand Wizard had stared at her for a long time and then left without saying a word. Miss Pinkerton frogmarched Ruby into her office.

"How, I would like to know, did two such brilliant magicians manage to have such a stupid daughter?" shouted Miss Pinkerton, going purple with rage.

"You have let me down, young lady, and the whole school as well," she yelled above the deafening noise of the chiming clocks. "I would like you to leave immediately, but unfortunately I find, much to my annoyance, that there is nowhere to send you. So, for the time being, you will have to stay here and help in the kitchen."

"It's not as bad as all that," said Lily later, trying to sound cheerful.

"How do you make that out?" said Ruby gloomily. "I'm no good at magic. I have just upset the Grand Wizard. The school is probably going to be shut down. I have to work in the kitchen, and to make matters worse, I won't ever get my lamp or wand back."

"If the school shuts down you can come home with me," said Lily brightly. "Mom and Dad would know what to do. I'm sure they could help."

"Thanks," said Ruby.

"I'm sure something will turn up," said Lily, trying to sound encouraging.

9

What turned up was as much a surprise to Ruby as it was to Miss Pinkerton. It seemed that Ruby had an uncle.

Ruby's uncle was a large, jolly man who looked like an actor in need of a theater.

"I have searched the four corners of the globe to find my little niece, and here she is, hidden away in your excellent school," he boomed to Miss Pinkerton. "Allow me to introduce myself. I am the Great Alfonso, brother of the late Mr. Genie, and devoted uncle of Ruby Genie." He looked a little taken aback by the sight of Ruby.

"Are you telling me, Miss Pinkerton, that this wee girl is ten? She looks more like six to my untrained eye. What have you done, starved her?"

Miss Pinkerton looked flustered. "No, no such thing. Ruby has just gotten smaller, all of her own accord. Nothing, I can assure you, to do with us."

"Oh, my poor little niece," said Alfonso. "Tell me, what have they done to you?"

Ruby wasn't sure what to say. Miss Pinkerton was glaring at her.

"Never mind," said Alfonso. "Put it all behind you. We have the future in front of us." He paused, then said, "The lamp, where is the lamp?"

Miss Pinkerton looked quite put out.

"I feel that as Ruby has caused us so much trouble and expense, the lamp is a small price to pay for her school fees."

Alfonso's face clouded over. "You toy with me, the Great Alfonso, at your peril," he said. "My brother's lamp in exchange for a stay at your school! Madam, have you completely lost your marbles? That lamp is priceless," he said, putting an arm around Ruby. "Priceless to us, his only remaining family."

Miss Pinkerton looked suddenly defeated and handed over the lamp. As Alfonso took it from her, the frown lifted from his face. He waved his arms and the lamp vanished into his coat. Ruby looked on, amazed.

"My mother's wand," she whispered to Alfonso. Miss Pinkerton realized she had met her match. She went over to her desk and handed the wand to Alfonso. In the twinkling of an eye, the wand vanished too.

"How do you do that?" said Ruby, really impressed.

"Later, my dear child, later." He turned and bowed to Miss Pinkerton. "I hope, dear lady," he said, taking her hand and kissing it, "that with a little extra tuition Ruby will soon be taking up her place again at Grimlocks."

Miss Pinkerton looked doubtful and was about to say so when she was rudely interrupted by all the clocks striking twelve.

10

"Is that your tummy rumbling or distant thunder?" said Alfonso merrily as they were driving away from Grimlocks.

"It's my tummy," said Ruby. "It seems like ages since I've eaten."

"Well then, lunch is the order of the day."

They stopped at a little café. Alfonso ordered a huge plate of scrambled eggs, tea, toast, scones, jam and cream, plus an extra plate of cream cakes.

"Eat up, my dear girl. There's plenty more where that came from."

Ruby was still uncertain what to make of her newly acquired uncle. He seemed pleasant enough. She knew he had a temper because she had seen how he'd behaved toward Miss Pinkerton—not that she didn't deserve it. The most important thing was that he'd gotten back the lamp and wand, so he couldn't be all bad, could he?

"You don't look one little bit like my father," she said, feeling braver.

"No, my dear little girl," said Alfonso. "We were as different as chalk and cheese. Alas, your father was the golden boy—I had nothing like his talents. However, I hope I don't over-flatter myself by saying that I am now a magician to be reckoned with."

"I wonder why my father never said anything about you," said Ruby.

"It breaks my heart," said Alfonso, "to remember these sad things, but when your father and I were little boys, we would fight, as boys do. I am sorry to say I was jealous of him. To my everlasting regret, we fell out and I swore I would never see him again. So many years have passed; so much water has flowed under the bridge ... When I heard of his tragic end, it broke my heart, dear girl."

He brought out a large spotted hanky and blew his nose like a trumpet. The little café went quiet, and everyone turned to look.

"You see, dear girl," he said, "they all recognize the Great Alfonso." He had now lost all interest in talking about anything other than himself, a subject he knew a lot about.

It was early in the evening when they arrived in Fizzlewick. Ruby was pleased to see Alfonso lived above a small magic shop. As he parked outside she caught glimpses of all sorts of interesting boxes and books, cloaks and hats in the window.

Above the door a painted sign creaked in the wind. It read:

ALFONSO
SpELS AnD MaJiC

"Excuse me," said Ruby, "why does your sign say—"

"Wonderful, isn't it?" interrupted Alfonso. "I painted it myself. I bought the shop off an old magician friend of mine, after a fortune cookie prophesied 'the door to your future is in a basement.' I like a good riddle, my dear child!"

Ruby was baffled. "Why did you buy this shop if your future lay in a basement?" she asked.

"Well, my friend said the shop had gotten the better of him," said Alfonso. "There was a door in the basement that wouldn't open. He was convinced there was some great secret behind it. He tried everything to get it open, and in the end he decided to give up and retire to the seaside. When I heard the words 'door' and 'basement', I knew I must buy the shop. One should never underestimate a fortune cookie!" said Alfonso grandly.

"And have you opened the door in the basement?" asked Ruby.

"That's quite enough questions for one day, dear girl," said Alfonso, sounding a little irritated. Ruby didn't dare ask anything else.

And that was how Ruby found herself living in an apartment over a magic shop.

11

To begin with, everything seemed to go well. It was a lot more exciting than being at Grimlocks. Alfonso was generosity itself. On Ruby's first day he took her shopping at the department store of wonders and spells, and made a great show of choosing her a dress.

"You can't wear that school uniform anymore, child," said Alfonso. "It clashes with the décor."

Ruby tried on dress after dress until Alfonso found one he liked, a pink frock with a huge bow.

"Now you look like my niece, dear heart," said Alfonso.

Ruby hadn't liked her school uniform one little bit, but she liked the pink frock even less. She wanted to say so, but Alfonso wasn't listening. He was thinking about what a great actor he was, and how well he played the part of a generous and caring uncle, which of course could not have been further from the truth.

Alfonso had followed the careers of Mr. Genie and his wife Myrtle with starstruck envy. He had seen amazing things happen when the lovely Mrs. Genie waved her magic wand, and watched the audience gasp in wonder as Mr. Genie wafted out of his magic lamp. So when he heard of their untimely deaths, he saw his chance. If only he could get his hands on that lamp and that wand, how his life would change! He too would become a great magician. He would be the Great Alfonso!

Alfonso was all prepared to spend his life

savings on buying the lamp and the wand when he heard that they had been given to the Genies' only child, Ruby. He didn't even know they had a child! She must have great magical powers—that was why they had kept so quiet about her. But he needed that lamp and wand more than Ruby did . . .

That was why Alfonso decided to pretend to be Ruby's uncle and abduct her from Grimlocks School. It had worked like a dream. Miss Pinkerton, the old cabbage leaf, had believed every word he'd said. Now he had Ruby, and, far more importantly, he had the lamp and the wand. Alfonso was not going to waste any more time.

12

Ruby couldn't understand what she had done wrong. Alfonso became like an actor taking off his disguise. Gone was the kind and generous uncle who wanted his niece to look her very best—all gone in a puff of blue smoke. In his place there appeared a frightening, bad-tempered man. Ruby could see quite clearly now that this was not her uncle.

"I've had enough of this playacting. It's time for you to earn your keep," said Alfonso. He took the lamp and the wand out of his safe and placed them carefully on a table. He could hardly contain his excitement.

"Now show me the mysteries of the lamp," he said, rubbing his chubby hands together in glee.

Ruby looked at him, amazed. "I don't know what you mean," she said.

Alfonso laughed. "Oh, very funny! Well, if you like you can start by showing me how the wand performs, and we can move on to the lamp later."

"Honest, I don't know anything about them. They weren't mine, they belonged to my mother and father," said Ruby, rather worried by the glint in Alfonso's eye.

"I know that, you stupid little girl," said Alfonso. "That's why I wanted them. You must know what to do. Otherwise, why would your parents have left them to you?"

"I don't know," said Ruby, her eyes pricking with tears.

"Oh, very touching. I weep for you, I sympathize. Now, no more fun and games," said Alfonso. He was turning redder and redder.

"I'd like to help, but I'm no good at magic," said Ruby, her legs shaking.

"You are toying with the Great Alfonso. You play with me at your peril! Do you think that I would have invested all this time in you if I thought for one miserable moment that you couldn't make the lamp and the wand work?" said Alfonso furiously. "Well, don't just stand there, give the lamp a rub!"

Ruby rubbed the lamp with all her might, but nothing happened.

"I'm sorry," said Ruby, tears pouring down her face. Alfonso let out a cruel laugh. She tried waving the wand around. Nothing happened, except that Ruby was so frightened that she began to shrink.

Alfonso looked a little surprised, but said, "Now you see what the Great Alfonso can do when his anger is roused!"

Ruby too was surprised to find quite how much she had shrunk. She was now about as tall as the table. She climbed up onto a chair and tried again. Nothing happened, except that she could see her frightened face shining back at her in the lamp.

Alfonso's face had gone purple. His eyes looked as if they might pop out of his head.

"This is too much. You're playing with me!" yelled Alfonso, stamping his foot.

Oh dear, thought Ruby. I'm shrinking again.

"Do you think that I, the Great Alfonso, would have gone to so much trouble, pretending to be your uncle, squandering money on you, if I had known for one minute what a stupid, useless little worm you would turn out to be—"

Here Alfonso stopped and stared at Ruby. She had shrunk to about six inches.

"Now you see the spells I can cast on little girls who don't do what they're told!" shouted Alfonso. "You're useless!"

And he picked Ruby up and threw her inside an old handbag that was lying around. With one click it snapped shut and Ruby's world went dark. "Good riddance to bad rubbish!" yelled

Alfonso, and he flung open the window and
hurled the bag out.

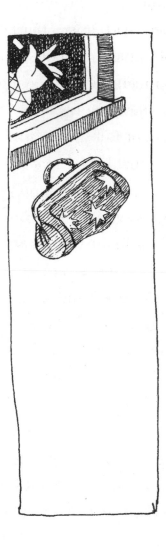

Ruby felt herself flying through the air. She tumbled over something in the dark, hurting her knee and hitting her head on something hard. Then Ruby knew no more.

Just then, a lady who had been buying a trick at the magic shop walked out onto the sidewalk.

She was surprised to see a handbag falling out of the sky. With one nifty move she caught it, then looked up to see if someone had dropped it by mistake.

"Is this yours?" she called to Alfonso as he was shutting the window.

"No, madam," said Alfonso. "What would I want with a handbag?"

"Imagine that!" said Aunt Hat (for that was the lady's name). "It must be my lucky day. This bag could come in very handy."

Just how handy, she was about to find out.

13

When Ruby woke up, she had no idea how long she had been in the handbag. She had lost all sense of time. All she knew was that she was hungry and frightened. Perhaps she had been forgotten, left on a shelf in Alfonso's magic shop. It would be years before anyone thought to look inside the bag. When they did, they would find a tiny skeleton.

Ruby started to cry. This was really bad. Worse than being an orphan, worse than Grimlocks, worse than being with Alfonso.

Suddenly the clasp of the bag flew open. Ruby could see daylight and a string of ladies' underpants hanging on a clothesline.

Aunt Hat was in a cheerful mood. Not every day, she thought, do you get given a handbag, even if it does come flying at you out of the sky. She got out a dust rag. "With a little polish," she said to herself, "that bag will look as good as new."

It is hard to know who was more startled when she opened the handbag, Ruby or Aunt Hat. It is true to say both were in for a very big surprise. What Ruby saw was a round, kind face staring down at her. What Aunt Hat saw nearly made her jump out of her skin. It's not every day you find a teeny-weeny little girl in a handbag.

Ruby's luck was about to change. Of all the people she could have landed on, she couldn't have chosen better than Aunt Hat. She lived in a small apartment that was full of odds and ends, colors and flowers. Everything had been put together in a higgledy-piggledy way that gave the place a warm, comfortable feeling. Ruby, for the first time in a long while, felt safe.

They sat together drinking tea at Aunt Hat's kitchen table. Ruby perched on a dollhouse chair, drinking from a tiny cup and saucer, while Aunt Hat cut her small slices of toast and cake.

Ruby was beginning to feel better already. She told Aunt Hat all about her adventure and how she had come to be in the bag in the first place. Aunt Hat's sunny face clouded over when Ruby came to the bit about Alfonso. She was horrified to learn that he had taken her so easily from Grimlocks. What was Miss Pinkerton thinking, letting Ruby go off with that dreadful old magician? What was the world of magic coming to? That's what she would like to know.

"I don't think I'll ever see my father's lamp or my mother's wand again," said Ruby sadly. "I wish I was good at magic like them. All I can do is read, and that's not much use."

"You can read! Oh petal, that is some magic trick!" said Aunt Hat, really impressed. "That is something I've never been able to do."

"Really?" said Ruby.

"Oh yes, petal, to be able to read is worth more than old lamps and wands," said Aunt Hat. "If I could read properly, I might have been able to find myself another job after the magic left me."

"I don't understand," said Ruby.

Aunt Hat laughed. "I haven't introduced my-self properly. I am Aunt Hat, a children's con-jurer." She pointed toward a beautiful collection of hats hanging on the wall. "That's how I got my name, on account of the wonderful hats I wore. When I was a bit younger than I am now I was a rather good children's entertainer, but something happened, and I lost my magic touch. These days I'm grateful for any little job that comes my way."

"That's very sad. What are you going to do?" asked Ruby.

"I can only do my best with my fisherman's vest," said Aunt Hat cheerfully. "As it happens

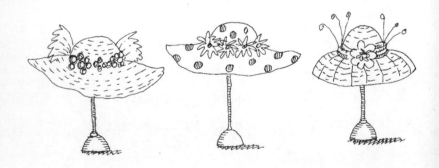

I'm booked to do a children's party tomorrow, because Cecil the Snake Man has come down with the flu. But I have a feeling that now I've met you, Ruby Genie, maybe, just maybe, things might get better."

14

That night Ruby slept in Aunt Hat's bedroom, in a little dollhouse, on a wrought iron bed with a feather mattress and feather pillows. Ruby read Aunt Hat *Aladdin* for a bedtime story. For the first time in ages she went to sleep happy.

The next day the sun shone through the windows, and the apartment twinkled in the sunny light. Aunt Hat was busy making tiny pancakes for breakfast. She had laid a miniature table with dollhouse plates and cutlery. In the middle of the table was a small bunch of glass flowers.

After breakfast, Aunt Hat found a box of dolls' clothes for Ruby to look through.

"I have boxes and boxes of useless small things, don't ask me why! I just love collecting dollhouse dolls and furniture." Aunt Hat laughed merrily. "I must have known that one day I would meet you."

Ruby had hated the clothes Alfonso had bought for her and made her wear, so she was thrilled to be able to look through Aunt Hat's boxes of delights. She finally chose a hat with bells hanging from it with a tiny spoon sewn onto the front, a pair of baggy trousers, and a very beautiful old coat covered in stars. It was almost as if it had been made for her.

"Don't you look wonderful!" said Aunt Hat. "Quite the magician, if you don't mind me saying."

That afternoon Ruby went with Aunt Hat
to the children's birthday party. Aunt Hat had
gone to considerable trouble to clean out the
handbag. She had removed the bit of old orange
peel that had been left in there and now the
bag shone inside and out. Ruby sat on a dollhouse armchair so that she would be comfortable while traveling. She had a flashlight so she
could see in the dark and a ladder so she could
climb up and look out.

The party was held in a very grand house on Canal Street. A rather over-anxious mother greeted Aunt Hat.

"Oh hello," she said. "You haven't come a moment too soon. The little darlings have gotten through all the games and demolished Pin the Tail on the Donkey, and now they want entertaining before lunch."

Aunt Hat was shown into a sitting room where a stage had been set up. A little girl in a huge pink frilly dress came over. She looked like a marshmallow on legs.

"Here is the birthday girl," said the mother in a flustered voice. "Charlotte, say hello to Aunt Hat."

"Oh Mommy," said Charlotte in disgust. "I thought you'd gotten the snake man. You know, the one Miranda had at her party. She got to hold a tarantula."

"Now precious," said her mother, "you know he isn't well. We were very lucky to get Aunt Hat."

Charlotte stamped her foot on the floor.

"I don't want Aunt Hat. She's for babies!" And Charlotte stomped out of the room, slamming the door behind her. Her mother gave a nervous little laugh.

"She's just a little over-excited. You know how it is. They wait all year for this day, and we do so want to get it right."

Aunt Hat was left alone to set up. She opened

the bag so that Ruby could see out. In no time at all the room filled up with noisy giggling girls in party dresses.

"I had a sword swallower for my party," said one little girl with a pink bow.

"That's nothing," said a girl in blue. "I had a fire eater at mine. He lay on a bed of nails and I got to stand on him. When he got up there were real nail marks all down his back."

Aunt Hat tried to get their attention but nobody seemed in the least bit interested in what she was doing. Ruby had by now climbed up her little ladder so that she could see what was going on. She had to agree that Aunt Hat was pretty terrible.

"I know how you do that!" shouted one girl from the front. Charlotte's parents were now in quite a state as the noise of bored children rose to a deafening din.

"I could do better myself," said her father crossly.

"She was all I could get at such short notice," the mother snapped back. The birthday girl burst into tears.

"This is the worst birthday ever," she sobbed.

Her mother turned desperately to Aunt Hat. "Do something, anything, for goodness' sake!" she wailed.

15

What happened next not only silenced the whole party but took Aunt Hat completely by surprise. Hidden in the handbag, Ruby wanted to help Aunt Hat so badly that she felt she was going to burst. She couldn't bear the idea of all these children not liking Aunt Hat's magic show. She could see tears in Aunt Hat's eyes as the children began to jeer. They shouldn't make fun of such a kind friend! If only she could do something to help—anything—like make lots of sweets appear! She closed her eyes and concentrated. As she did so, she felt a tingle go through her whole body. It was then that Ruby realized two things: First, the room seemed to have gone very quiet, and second, and far more amazing, Ruby Genie was doing her first ever magic trick.

The children watched as the first few sweets flew up in the air. They stopped when Aunt Hat put her bag on the table. It's difficult to make sweets appear when you're wobbling around in a handbag. The children began to shout, "We want more! We want more!" Then a fountain of sweets shot out like fireworks, in all directions and in all different colors.

When the display finished, Aunt Hat was so astonished she couldn't think of what to say.

The children clapped and cheered. "More! More!" they shouted again.

Aunt Hat looked in the bag. Inside she saw Ruby Genie with a huge smile on her face, and the beginnings of a birthday cake. Aunt Hat had just enough time to say, "For my grand finale," before the birthday cake came floating out of the bag. Aunt Hat caught it with great aplomb. (That was one thing Aunt Hat had always been good at, catching things.)

The cake was followed by a shower of blazing candles that formed the words "Happy Birthday" in the air before shooting down like darts to position themselves in the icing.

"How did you do that?" asked Charlotte.

Aunt Hat laughed. "The secret is in the bag," she said.

After that the party was a great success. At going home time, Charlotte looked a little sheepish as she said to Aunt Hat that it was the best magic show she had ever seen. All her friends wanted Aunt Hat to entertain at their parties. In fact, Charlotte's parents were so pleased with the way things had gone that they paid Aunt Hat extra.

That night Aunt Hat and Ruby went home in a taxi.

16

The next few weeks were a whirlwind of children's parties. Ruby was really enjoying herself. She liked nothing better than being hidden in the bag. It gave her all the courage she needed, knowing no one could see her doing her magic.

At first, she could only make sweets and cakes appear. Aunt Hat wouldn't have minded one little bit if she had just stuck to that, for all the children loved them.

But Aunt Hat had a feeling that sweets were just the beginning. Ruby had worked out that as long as she had a picture of what she wanted in her head, she could usually make it appear. At first floating unformed out of the bag, in no time it took on the shape of whatever Ruby was imagining.

The children in the audience knew nothing about Ruby. What they saw was Aunt Hat waving her wand and making the most magical things appear from her bag. Sometimes things appeared even when she wasn't waving her wand. The truth was that Aunt Hat was never quite sure what Ruby would come up with next, whether it would last any length of time or vanish at once in a puff of rainbow smoke.

Every day Ruby's magic got stronger and her confidence grew. There were a few teething problems, like the time she imagined a snake with two hundred legs that made all the children scream and run. The parents laughed nervously and looked most relieved when it vanished, but Aunt Hat didn't mind a bit. That was what Ruby loved about Aunt Hat. Whatever she came up with, Aunt Hat would say, when they were safely home, "Well, wasn't that amazing! Aren't you the cleverest magician ever!"

Aunt Hat had had the bright idea of sewing a secret compartment into the bag, where Ruby could hide. The grand finale of every show came when Aunt Hat lifted up the bag so all the children could see that it was quite empty. No one knew about Ruby, and that was the way both of them wanted it to stay.

17

Aunt Hat's magic handbag was becoming the talk of the town. It wasn't only children who wanted to see her magic show. Offers began to pour in from around the world: Paris offered her the Opera House to star in; New York, the Met; London, Covent Garden. All were willing to pay amounts of money Aunt Hat had only dreamed of. Aunt Hat was becoming quite a star. Her picture appeared on the front page of the *Wizards' World*. The headline read: AUNT HAT—THE MOST EXTRAORDINARY MAGICIAN EVER! OR IS THE SECRET IN THE BAG?

Everyone wanted to know how the magic was done, and more to the point, how had such a hopeless magician as Aunt Hat become an overnight sensation?

But things were getting a little out of control. It was like winning the lottery, only better and a bit more worrying.

Aunt Hat was right to worry that with all this attention, sooner or later, she would come to the notice of a certain somebody, and it wouldn't take this certain somebody long to work out the secret of the magic bag. When that happened, Aunt Hat knew that Ruby would be in great danger.

Ruby was blissfully unaware of Aunt Hat's worries or the razzmatazz that was surrounding them. She was enjoying being with Aunt Hat and finding out about the fun in magic. She had never felt happier. She had even stopped worrying about whether the magic was due to her or the bag. Aunt Hat was right, it didn't matter.

But now that they had been asked to perform in such grand theaters Ruby felt the time
had come to see if she could fly. After all, her
father and mother both could. She had been
practicing for the past week. It was lucky that
Aunt Hat was so good at catching, otherwise
Ruby might really have come to grief.

She was forever launching herself off the
ends of tables, convinced that this time she
would defy gravity and fly, but she had no

success. She must be doing something wrong. Her father had been able to waft out of his lamp like a true genie should, as well as walking on two legs like everybody else. Her mother had also been good at flying, though she never did it in polite society. Flying, she used to say, is so theatrical and looks out of place in a sitting room. Ruby wondered whether, if she still had her father's lamp, she would be able to waft or if she had her mother's wand would she be able to fly?

It wasn't long before the Great Alfonso saw the pictures of Aunt Hat and her famous bag. At first he took little notice. The rumors he had heard about Aunt Hat were too far-fetched to be believed. He knew for a fact that Aunt Hat was useless at magic. There must be some mistake, of that he was sure. Why, the other day, she had been spotted talking to this bag!

"As mad as a hairbrush," Alfonso had chuckled to himself. That was before he'd seen the pictures in the newspaper.

Alfonso's chuckle turned to rage. Why, that was *his* bag, and that must be Ruby Genie doing the magic. How dare that good-for-nothing little twerp treat him, the Great Alfonso, so badly! He would get her back and this time Ruby would do as she was told. She would make that lamp work if it was the last thing she ever did.

18

Miss Pinkerton was in one of her rare good moods. The Grand Wizard had said he wanted to make another visit to the school. Much to her surprise and relief, it seemed he had been most impressed last time he was there. Miss Pinkerton was positively purring with delight. Thank goodness, she thought to herself, that I got rid of that troublesome Ruby Genie. What on earth possessed me to give that child a scholarship? Miss Fisher was right, it was probably the reading that had ruined her. But now all that was safely behind them. The main thing was that the Grand Wizard was clearly, although somewhat unexpectedly, pleased with the talent displayed by the other pupils. Congratulations were in order, of that she was sure.

But, oh dear me, poor Miss Pinkerton was in for a nasty shock.

The Grand Wizard looked as though he would explode with rage when Miss Pinkerton, in a cheerful voice, told him that Ruby Genie was no longer at the school. He looked so cross, in fact, that for one moment Miss Pinkerton feared she would be turned into a toad.

"You have done what?" he shouted. "I thought you were looking after her! Instead, you let her go off with a man you have never set eyes on before, who claims to be her uncle! What on earth possessed you?"

Miss Pinkerton was taken aback. "He seemed like a very nice man, I thought. Ruby is a lucky girl to have such a caring uncle."

"Miss Pinkerton," said the Grand Wizard slowly, trying to contain his anger. "Am I hearing you right? You let a ten-year-old orphan go off with a complete stranger because he told you he was her uncle and he *seemed* like a nice man?"

Miss Pinkerton looked worried. "I thought it was for the best, her being so bad at magic and always having her nose stuck in a book."

She had hardly finished speaking when the Grand Wizard let out a growl. "You thought, did you! The stars save us from any more of your ghastly thoughts. Did he take the lamp and the wand too?"

"Yes," admitted Miss Pinkerton a little sheepishly. "Though I did try to suggest that we keep them as payment for her schooling."

The Grand Wizard raised his bushy eyebrows in disbelief. "Oh really! Do I make myself clear when I tell you that Ruby has no uncles? He wanted Ruby because he saw something you have woefully failed to see—that Ruby is destined to become one of the great genies of our time."

"But Grand Wizard," said Miss Pinkerton feebly, "when you came to our Open Day you seemed rather disappointed with Ruby."

The Grand Wizard said very slowly, as if talking to a three-year-old, "On the contrary, Miss Pinkerton. I was amazed to see her there. I came today to see how you were managing. But what do I find? No Ruby!"

Miss Pinkerton was lost for words. "Are you sure," she said, trying to look on the bright side, "that we are talking about the same girl? I mean, you don't think you're muddling her up with her friend Lily?"

"No, Miss Pinkerton," said the Grand Wizard, "I have not muddled her up with anyone. Ruby Genie was the girl I saw trying, if I remember correctly, to pull a rabbit from a hat."

"Yes," said Miss Pinkerton, puffing herself up, "and failing."

"Yes, failing to pull a miserable rabbit from a hat, but doing something far more extraordinary—shrinking."

Miss Pinkerton turned white and sat down heavily on a chair.

"Oh dear, I didn't think anything of it, I mean it wasn't the first time . . ." Her voice trailed off as all the clocks began to chime the hour. The Grand Wizard frowned and raised his hand. The room was silent.

"Quite," said the Grand Wizard. "Not even her vain and silly parents had seen what a wonderful little genie she would turn out to be. I was impressed that you had spotted a very gifted child. Even Wizodean Academy had failed to see her talent. I thought I had underestimated you as a headmistress. I was delighted that you had given her a scholarship. And when you assured me she was in good hands, I was doubly pleased."

"Oh dear me," whimpered Miss Pinkerton. "What have I done?"

"What indeed," said the Grand Wizard. "Do you have any idea how powerful that lamp is? Once its power is roused, Ruby could be caught in it forever. Due to your woeful stupidity, Ruby Genie is now in great danger."

19

The plan was so simple that it made the Great Alfonso smile. It would be like stealing candy from a baby.

Aunt Hat had just finished performing her magic show at a house on Market Street. As usual a crowd of people were waiting for autographs. It was then that Alfonso made his move.

"Madam, that is my handbag," he said loudly.

Aunt Hat took no notice. Alfonso wasn't the least put out.

"Lady, I was talking to you. That is my bag! You stole it from me."

The crowd let out a gasp. Aunt Hat looked flustered.

"I want my bag back," said Alfonso, and he grabbed hold of the bag and to Aunt Hat's astonishment began to walk away with it, as cool as a cucumber.

"Come back!" she yelled. "You have no right to take my bag!"

The crowd ran after Alfonso. A large man took the bag from him and handed it to Aunt Hat.

"Oh thank you," said Aunt Hat, much relieved. Alfonso glared at her.

"I, the Great Alfonso, accuse you of being nothing more than a common thief," he said.

"That's absurd!" said Aunt Hat.

"Now look here, my good man, that's no way to talk to a lady," said a gentleman in the crowd.

"Quite right," said another.

"Well!" said the large man who had rescued the bag from Alfonso. "There is a simple way to solve this problem. The judge can sort it out."

The judge was rather surprised to see her courtroom fill up with so many people. She was even more surprised by Alfonso's claims that this famous handbag had once belonged to him.

"You have accused Miss Hat of stealing this handbag. Would you please tell the court how it came to be stolen in the first place?"

"With pleasure," said Alfonso. Here he was, the Great Alfonso, center stage, with everyone looking at him. What bliss!

"That woman," he said in a theatrical voice, "took my bag from me, just after I'd finished doing a special piece of magic, which involved creating a genie to put inside it." He paused and sighed. "I was, as you can imagine, exhausted after my exertions. I put the bag on the windowsill. Unfortunately a gust of wind blew it off, and it fell onto the street below. It was caught by that woman there. I asked, nay, I begged her to give it back but she ran off with it down the street. I tried to go after her, but by the time I got downstairs to the street she was gone." Alfonso blew his nose loudly and dabbed his eyes. "That woman has robbed the Great Alfonso of his fortune and his fame. I assure you that without my magic, that bag is worthless."

There was silence in the court. "This is a very serious accusation," said the judge to Aunt Hat. "How do you defend yourself?"

Aunt Hat stood up. "I didn't steal the bag. I would never do such a thing. It is true that the bag was thrown from Alfonso's window and that I caught it. I asked him if it is was his and he said 'No, what would I want with a hand-bag?' Those were his very words. I took it home and the rest is history."

"The true owner of the bag will know what it contains," said the judge. "Mr. Alfonso, please tell the court what was in the bag."

"Nothing," said Alfonso grandly. "Only a small genie and all my hopes and dreams."

The magistrate looked in the bag. She could see nothing. She put her hand in the bag. She could feel nothing. She turned the bag upside down. No genie. Ruby was well hidden.

"The bag may well contain all your hopes and dreams, Mr. Alfonso, but it has no genie in it," said the magistrate. "As far as I can see, it is completely empty. Miss Hat, would you like to tell the court what you had in the bag?"

"Oh, nothing much," said Aunt Hat. "A hanky, a purse, a hat and of course a hatstand, a table and chair, a teapot, cups and saucers, and don't forget the plate of cakes. Did I mention the candlesticks? Then of course there's my umbrella—one is never sure what the weather will do. And oh dear, I nearly forgot the pond and the ducks. I can't go anywhere without them."

"This is ridiculous. This woman is making fun of the law," said Alfonso.

The judge opened the bag for the second time. "There is, as I said, nothing in this bag."

"There must be some mistake," said Aunt Hat. "I know for a fact that I put those things in this morning. Well, wait a moment. I might have left my purse at home after all. I do hope not."

All this time, Ruby had been hiding in her secret compartment, trying not to be seen or felt. She had been quite joggled about when the judge had tipped the bag upside down.

The judge was about to give her verdict when, to her astonishment, a purse came flying out of the bag.

"Oh good," said Aunt Hat. "I thought I hadn't left it at home."

The courtroom soon filled up with a hat-stand, a table laid for tea, a plate of cakes, three candlesticks, a pond complete with ducks and weeds, and last of all, a large hanky that flew straight into Aunt Hat's pocket. A loud cheer went up for Aunt Hat.

The case was about to be dismissed when Miss Pinkerton came charging in.

"Arrest that man!" she shouted at the top of her voice, pointing at Alfonso. Then she marched right into the duckpond.

The judge looked taken aback. "Order in the court!" she said. "Order!"

Miss Pinkerton, her mouth full of pond

weeds, cried out again, "Arrest that man! He has abducted a child!"

In the chaos that followed, the Great Alfonso disappeared and so did Aunt Hat's bag.

20

Aunt Hat had never felt so miserable. She had lost Ruby, the one little person she loved. What was she going to do? And, more importantly, how was she going to get Ruby back? She would have to work out a plan. Alfonso must be stopped before he did anything dreadful.

"No time for lunch. It's time for action," said Aunt Hat to an empty kitchen.

"That's a pity," came back a small voice. "I was feeling quite hungry."

Aunt Hat couldn't believe her eyes. There, standing on the kitchen table, was Ruby. "Oh my petal, it's you, it really is you! How did you do it?"

"Well," said Ruby, feeling rather pleased with herself, "I flew. I was so scared of being taken away by Alfonso, I just hid under the hanky, and concentrated very hard, hoping it would work, and thank goodness, it did!"

Never had two people been more pleased to see each other. They sat drinking tea and eating chocolate cake and talking about what to do next.

"Why do you think Miss Pinkerton turned up?" said Ruby.

"I suppose," said Aunt Hat, "because she felt guilty at having let you go off with Alfonso in the first place."

"Silly old Miss Pinkerton," laughed Ruby. "It served her right when she fell into the duck-pond, with the weeds and the ducks all flapping around."

"I had no idea that pond was so deep," said Aunt Hat. "Now, down to serious business. What are we going to do about Alfonso? As soon as he realizes you aren't inside the bag, he's going to come looking for you."

"Why?" asked Ruby. "I can't make the lamp work, or the wand either. I don't know how."

"I don't think the lamp and the wand matter anymore," said Aunt Hat. "He just wants you because you're so amazing at magic."

Ruby looked worried. "I don't think it's anything to do with me. I think the magic is in the bag."

"Let's find out," said Aunt Hat. "See if you can make some sweets appear without the bag, my petal."

Ruby tried her hardest, but nothing happened. "It's no good," she said, looking very small and sad.

"Well, this will never do. What right has that old buffoon to go around taking things that aren't his?" said Aunt Hat, putting on her hat and coat. "We'll just have to go to his apartment and get the bag back, and while we're about it we'll get the lamp and the wand too."

That evening, under cover of darkness, they set out for Alfonso's magic shop. Ruby traveled in Aunt Hat's pocket. Fortunately no one was around to see them break in.

The shop was scary, full of jars filled with sinister-looking things and masks that looked like real faces in the darkness. Aunt Hat tripped over something and it made a loud noise, like a clap of thunder.

"Oh pants!" she whispered. "We're in for it now!"

They waited, half expecting the lights to go on and Alfonso to be standing there, but all was quiet.

"He keeps the lamp and the wand upstairs in a safe," said Ruby. Aunt Hat shined a flashlight to light the way.

Alfonso's room looked as if a hurricane had struck it. He had obviously had one of his fa-mous tantrums. Everything in it had been bro-ken or smashed. Aunt Hat picked up the bag. It was quite battered and turned inside out. Then she tripped over the lamp, which had been

thrown carelessly on the floor. Aunt Hat put Ruby and the lamp on the one remaining table for safekeeping, and started looking for the wand.

21

"What a touching scene!" Alfonso's voice boomed in the quiet room. Aunt Hat nearly jumped out of her skin and dropped the flashlight. Alfonso turned the lights on.

"Don't move," he said. "I've got you both now."

He made a grab for Ruby. "Well, isn't this Alfonso's lucky day?"

"Oh pants," said Aunt Hat as Alfonso tied her up.

"I can now add housebreaking to your list of crimes," Alfonso chuckled. "As for you," he said to Ruby, "we have work to do. This time there is no playing with the Great Alfonso."

Just then there was a loud banging at the door. "Oh ramblasting!" said Alfonso. "I will not be disturbed!"

Holding Ruby tightly in one sweaty hand, and the lamp in the other, he climbed down the stairs to the basement. Ruby felt very frightened. Alfonso's footsteps echoed as if the basement went on forever.

Alfonso put Ruby on a workbench with the lamp next to her.

"Now, my dear little genie girl, make that lamp work."

Ruby closed her eyes and tried her best, but nothing happened.

"It will be the end of you, you miserable child, if you don't!" yelled Alfonso.

"I can't do magic without my bag," said Ruby bravely, though her teeth were chattering.

Alfonso grabbed her and rushed upstairs again, holding her tightly. The banging on the door was getting louder. There was not a minute to lose.

He picked up the bag.

"I can't do it without Aunt Hat either," said Ruby.

Alfonso didn't say a word. He untied Aunt Hat and took her back down to the basement. Now voices could be heard shouting, "Open up in the name of the law!"

Alfonso bolted the door so that no one could come in.

"I have, as always, been generosity itself," said Alfonso. "I have even let you have this ridiculous old cabbage leaf to help you. Now Ruby, for the last time, make that lamp work!"

Ruby couldn't. What she could do was make the lamp fly, but Alfonso was too quick for her.

He grabbed the bag and in his rage threw it at the cellar door.

As he did so the door began to glow. On it appeared the words:

The Land of Wonders: Enter at Your Peril

"What does it say?" shouted Alfonso, pointing at the letters.

"Enter at your peril," said Ruby faintly.

And as she spoke, the door swung open and a bright golden light shone out. There before them was an orchard of glass trees, hung with precious stones and sparkling like rainbows.

"I'm rich!" cried Alfonso. "Richer than all the kings in the world!" He stumbled toward the door like a drunken man.

Suddenly there was a wail, as if from the center of the earth, and a voice as sad as sorrow said, "You have no right to enter here."

"Yes I have," said Alfonso, standing on the

threshold. "A fortune cookie told me the door to my future lay in a basement."

The door slammed shut.

"No, no!" shouted Alfonso, pounding on it. He turned to Ruby. "Open it again! I order you to!"

"She doesn't know how," said Aunt Hat.

"Oh be quiet, you old cabbage leaf," said Alfonso.

The door began to glow again. More words appeared, this time in silver. To her surprise, Ruby read:

Come in, Ruby Genie. Welcome.

Ruby's fears vanished. All at once the door began to shrink down to her size. She turned the handle and the door opened to reveal the same orchard, but now all on a tiny scale.

"Get a move on, girl! There's no time to lose," said Alfonso. "If you're not back in five minutes with all the jewels you can carry, your precious Aunt Hat is in trouble."

Ruby walked though the door. A river of gold ran through the orchard and silver blossom fell in a cool breeze. Jewels of red, blue, green, and purple tinkled down from the trees. Ruby picked up as many as she could carry and put them in her pockets.

She was just about to leave when she saw a beautiful little flower, like a daisy, all made out of precious stones. It was perfect for Aunt Hat. Ruby bent down and picked it up, and as she did so a voice as sweet as happiness spoke to her.

"Ruby," said the voice, "all the magic you need is in you. You are loved."

22

"Give me the stones!" screamed Alfonso. "Stop playing around and give them to me!"

Ruby emptied her pockets and put all the tiny little stones on the workbench.

"That's it?" said Alfonso. "Is that all you could bring the Great Alfonso?"

He was interrupted by four policemen who came charging into the basement followed by Miss Pinkerton.

"Arrest that man!" ordered Miss Pinkerton. "He is responsible for the murder of Ruby Genie!"

"I think that's a little far-fetched," said Aunt Hat mildly. "Ruby is over there." She pointed to Ruby, who was standing on the workbench. Miss Pinkerton let out a piercing scream, as if she'd been stabbed.

"What have you done to her? She's so small!"

The policemen thought Miss Pinkerton had been wounded, and rushed to rescue her. In the confusion, Alfonso grabbed Ruby and popped her into her father's lamp. He held it up as if he was about to throw it.

"Out of my way," he shouted, "or the little girl gets it!"

Nobody could have known what would happen next.

23

Ruby felt her body becoming silver and liquid. A tingle rushed through her, as if she had turned into air. To her amazement she began to waft out of the lamp, and to the horror of everyone there, she said in a voice that didn't sound like her own, "I am the genie of the lamp."

Alfonso let out a terrible laugh and did a little jig.

"I want you to tie up all those nasty people, my dear genie. Then bring me all the larger stones!"

Aunt Hat looked on, stunned, as Ruby Genie began to grow. She got bigger and bigger until she filled the entire basement.

"The Great Alfonso commands the genie of the lamp!" said Alfonso in a grand voice. This was the moment he had been waiting for all his life. Now nothing could stop him from becoming one of the most powerful magicians ever. He turned to Aunt Hat, Miss Pinkerton, and the four policemen and said, "Now you see what the Great Alfonso can do when his anger is roused!"

Ruby didn't seem to be paying attention to Alfonso's words. She just hovered.

"Go on, do as I say!" ordered Alfonso, although he looked a little worried. This was not how things should be.

At that moment there was a sound like waves crashing on a stony beach. As if from nowhere the Grand Wizard appeared.

"Leave the lamp immediately, Ruby," said the Grand Wizard in a loud clear voice, "and get back inside the bag. If you do not, you will be the slave of that lamp forever."

"Mind your own business, you muddling old fool. This is my genie and there's nothing you can do about it," sneered Alfonso.

"Oh, isn't there?" said the Grand Wizard, who had had quite enough of Alfonso. He raised his hand and immediately Alfonso was frozen like a statue.

Ruby was still hovering half in and half out of the lamp.

"I don't think Ruby can get out," said Aunt Hat anxiously.

"What I need is the wand, and quickly," said the Grand Wizard. "Time is running out."

Aunt Hat pushed past the policemen and rushed upstairs. Alfonso's apartment was such a mess she didn't know where to look. Suddenly she saw something twinkling under a chair— the wand! She picked it up and ran back down to the basement. She was only just in time. Ruby was about to be sucked back into the lamp.

The Grand Wizard touched the lamp with the wand. There was a flash of lightning and the lamp shattered into a thousand pieces.

"Oh!" cried Aunt Hat. "What's happened to Ruby?"

"Try the bag," said the Grand Wizard.

Aunt Hat ran over to the bag. There, to her great relief, was Ruby, dazed, as small as ever,

but all in one piece. Beside her lay a tiny flower. It was the most beautiful thing Aunt Hat had ever seen.

"It's for you," said Ruby with a smile.

They both looked at the magic door. On it shimmered the words:

Good-bye, Ruby Genie! Your Troubles Are Over.

"What an extraordinary business," said Aunt Hat. "And what a good thing that you can read, Ruby. Alfonso didn't stand a chance."

24

Things worked out very well. Alfonso was stripped of all his magical powers, which weren't as many as he liked to think. He now works in a candy shop, having to be nice to children, which he hates.

Miss Pinkerton has given up teaching children. Instead, she runs obedience classes for dogs.

Madame Vanish vanished. Miss Fisher was sent to count peas in a frozen pea factory. Mr. Gaspard started a new life doing firework displays, which he was very good at.

The Grand Wizard was so impressed with the way Aunt Hat kept her wits about her that he could think of no one better to be headmistress of Grimlocks School. Aunt Hat wasn't sure if she would be any good at it, but the Grand Wizard was a wise man and he saw that Aunt Hat had a magical gift for bringing out the best in children.

He was right. Aunt Hat was a wonderful teacher and all her pupils did well. Ruby helped her learn to read and Aunt Hat made sure that all the children could read and write as well as do spells. Grimlocks was voted top of the league of all the schools of magic. Much more importantly, all the children were happy.

Ruby's friends were so pleased to see her again. Even if she was tiny, she was still great fun to be with. And here is the most surprising part. Ruby had always thought it was Alfonso's magic that made her tiny, though Aunt Hat had never believed the old windbag had that much magic in him. She, like Zack, was sure that Ruby had shrunk because she was so frightened, and this proved to be right. After only one term back with her schoolfriends, Ruby started to grow again, and in no time at all she was back to her old size.

Aunt Hat made sure that Ruby was kept out of harm's way, and the Grand Wizard put a protective spell on the school so that Ruby's magic was given space to grow.

Aunt Hat and Ruby spend the school holidays together, traveling. Ruby learned how to use a magic carpet, which meant they were able to fly off on wonderful adventures between terms.

As for the little jeweled flower, Aunt Hat put it in a glass box with some words written underneath:

All the magic you need
is in You.
You are loved.

Lest Ruby should ever forget.

It's time to
flip the book
for another
magical story!

It's time to
flip the book
for another
magical story!

The Boy
Who Could Fly

written and illustrated by

Sally Gardner

DIAL BOOKS FOR YOUNG READERS

★

For Dominic
with all my love

★

The Boy
Who Could Fly

1

Mrs. Top opened her front door one gray Wednesday afternoon to find a Fat Fairy standing there.

"Is this 6 Valance Road, and are you Thomas Top's mother?" asked the Fat Fairy.

Mrs. Top looked a little taken aback.

"Yes," she said, "but I think there must be some mistake. The birthday party has had to be postponed."

The Fat Fairy adjusted her glasses and huffed.

"Well. I have it written down here that I am

booked for today, the fourth of May, at three o'clock for Thomas Top's ninth birthday," said the Fat Fairy firmly. "And I never get it wrong."

"I don't understand. I didn't book anyone for Thomas's party. I mean, we always have Mr. Spoons the magician. I never asked for a fairy," said Mrs. Top.

"No one ever does, dear," said the Fat Fairy. "We are supposed to be a surprise."

Mrs. Top was beginning to feel quite flustered.

"You see, the party isn't happening today because Thomas is sick," she said. "We had to postpone it. He's going to have it on the same day as his dad's birthday now."

"Well, that is nothing to do with me," said the Fat Fairy. "I am here just to wish him a happy birthday. It says nothing about entertainment or parties."

"Oh I see," said Mrs. Top, feeling relieved, "you are some sort of singing telegram. I can't think who sent you."

"I wouldn't worry about it," said the Fat Fairy, smiling.

Thomas was propped up in bed. He felt terrible, with a sore throat and aching bones. A virus, the doctor had told his mom. He was to stay in bed until he felt better, and today was his birthday and he felt worse.

So far he had been given a book on fishing for beginners from his dad, a pen from his mom, a brown sweater from his aunt Maud, a set of colored markers from his friend Spud, and a quarter stuck with masses of tape to an old Christmas card from his uncle Alfie. Things were not looking good when suddenly his mom entered the room, with the fattest fairy he had ever seen.

She had bright pink hair and was wearing a tutu two sizes too small. Her wings were lopsided and it looked as if she had sat on her tiara. If Thomas hadn't been feeling so unwell he would have burst out laughing.

"It's a surprise," said his mom anxiously.

The Fat Fairy looked around the room and huffed, then went and sat on the end of Thomas's bed.

"I wouldn't get too close to him," said Mom. "He could be contagious."

The Fat Fairy took no notice and said in a mournful voice, "Love a cup of tea, dear."

Mrs. Top went downstairs, saying she wouldn't be a minute.

"Not much of a birthday," said the Fat Fairy, looking around Thomas's room and at his presents.

"Why are you here?" said Thomas.

"To give you a birthday wish," said the Fat Fairy.

"You're kidding, right?" said Thomas.

"No," said the Fat Fairy. "Come on, just tell me what your wish is, and then I can be on my way."

"I don't know," said Thomas. He wasn't sure what to make of her. "This is just a game, isn't it?"

"It's no game," said the Fat Fairy. "Come on, let's get this finished before your mom comes back with tea and cupcakes."

"I wish I was—" said Thomas.

"No good," interrupted the Fat Fairy. "You can't wish for all the money in the world or to turn Aunt Maud into a sheep. It just won't work like that. You have to wish for something like having the most beautiful hair or being able to sing like an angel, or being a whiz at computers. Get it?"

Thomas looked at her again. "Mom doesn't have any cupcakes," he said.

The fairy shrugged her wings. "Come on, come on," she said. "Concentrate. It's not every day you get a wish granted."

"All right. I wish that—" said Thomas.

"No good," the fairy interrupted. "You can't wish for your father to be fun. It has to do with you, Thomas," she said gently. "After all, today is your ninth birthday."

Thomas looked surprised. "How did you know I was going to wish for that?" he asked.

"Quick," said the Fat Fairy as Mom's footsteps were heard coming up the stairs.

Thomas said the first thing that came into his head. "I wish I could fly." Why he said that, he had no idea.

"Nice one," said the Fat Fairy, standing up just as Mom entered the room with two cups of tea and a plate of cupcakes.

"I'm all done and dusted, dear," said the Fat Fairy, giving a loud belch. "All this wishing plays havoc with my insides," she went on, gulping down the tea and putting three cupcakes in her handbag. "Well, I can't stay here all day enjoying myself."

And without so much as a good-bye, she made her way down the stairs. Mom followed, saying, "Wait a minute, I was wondering which company sent you," but by the time she had made it to the front door, the Fat Fairy had vanished.

8

Thomas went back to school the following Monday.

Monday was his worst day. There was gym, and Thomas hated gym. "Could I have a note saying that I've been sick?" he asked his mom.

"No," said his dad firmly. "If you are well enough to go back to school, young man, you are well enough to play games."

"I think, Alan, that's a bit hard," said his mom. "He hasn't been feeling very well."

"I am not having that boy babied anymore," said Dad. "We have had quite enough interruption to our routine."

So Thomas endured the torture that was gym. Miss Peach took no nonsense from her class. She had all the equipment out: the balance beam, the trampoline, the mats, even the dreaded jumping horse.

Everyone lined up, ready to jump over the horse. It usually went with a good rhythm, that is until it was Thomas's turn. Today would be no different, he thought miserably.

Thomas closed his eyes and started his run, waiting for the bump as he hit the horse, the shout that would be Miss Peach telling him he wasn't trying hard enough, and the laughter that would be his classmates.

Except that he didn't hit the horse, and all he heard was a loud gasp. When he opened his eyes he was amazed to find that he was about six feet off the ground.

Thomas landed in a heap on the other side of the horse.

"Thomas Top, what do you think you're doing?" said a shocked Miss Peach.

"Nothing, Miss Peach," said Thomas. "Just jumping."

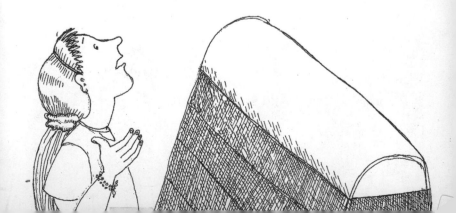

The class was silent. Children can jump high, but six feet off the ground was unbelievable! Miss Peach decided she was seeing things. Yes, that was it. She clapped her hands. "Now everyone, settle down and let's do it one more time. Well done, Thomas, for getting over the horse."

But it happened again. This time Thomas found himself about eight feet off the ground and heading for the other side of the gym. He landed with a loud thump.

"That's it, Thomas Top. I will not have this kind of showing off in my class," said Miss Peach. "You will go and sit outside until you calm down."

Thomas sat outside in the drafty corridor in his flimsy white T-shirt and brown shorts.

"What are you doing out here, Thomas Top?" said Mr. March, the headmaster.

"I got sent out for showing off," said Thomas apologetically.

Mr. March laughed. "That's not like you, Thomas. You're always such a quiet guy. Come on, let's see what this is all about."

The class was now on the trampoline.

"Sorry to interrupt, Miss Peach, but this little fellow tells me he's been sent outside for showing off. Is that right?"

"Yes," said Miss Peach flatly. "He was jumping too high."

Mr. March looked puzzled. "Jumping too high? Well, I never would have thought he had it in him."

"Neither would I," said Miss Peach, who did not appreciate the headmaster's interruption one little bit.

"Well," said Mr. March, "I'm sure Thomas will behave himself now, and perhaps he can join in on the trampoline."

Thomas had always hated the trampoline. He was no good at coordination; jumping up and down terrified the socks off him. He climbed up gingerly, his face pale.

"Don't forget to bend your knees," said Miss Peach sternly.

Thomas bent his knees and straightened up again, feeling very wobbly on his feet.

"He's not really trying, miss," said Suzi Morris.

"He didn't jump," said Joe Corry, another boy in his class. "He just bent his knees."

"He did jump. I saw him," said Thomas's loyal friend Spud.

"Now come on," said Mr. March. "I'm sure you can do better than that. Let's see you jump nice and high."

What happened next gave Thomas the biggest

shock of his life. He found himself going up
and up toward the ceiling of the gym, his legs
and arms flailing until he finally grabbed ahold
of a beam and hung there.

Thomas was scared of heights. They made
him feel sick. He was now higher than he had
ever been in his life, and he didn't know how it
had happened.

"Help! Please!" cried Thomas.

"Oh my word!" cried Mr. March. "Get a ladder, quick! Hold on, Thomas. We'll get you down."

But it was too late. Thomas felt his fingers getting weak. There was no way he was going to survive this. He was going to fall, break both his legs, his arms, his collarbone—everything. He let out a small scream, which was echoed by a much louder one from everyone below.

Thomas was falling like a stone.

He put out his arms to break
his fall—but that just made him
go up again! This couldn't be happening. He felt like he was on a roller
coaster. Perhaps it was all a bad dream.
He would wake up in a minute and find
himself safely back in bed with a nice safe
sore throat.

Instead he found himself sitting on a beam high up in the rafters, looking down at his class and teacher, who were all staring up at him, openmouthed. He hung on for dear life while Mr. March quickly ushered all the kids out of the gym.

"That's all fine and good," said Miss Peach to herself, "but the question is, how are we going to get him down?"

3

Mrs. Top arrived at the school in a terrible state. "What kind of incident? Why have I been called here?" she said. "I have already had to take a week off of work with Thomas being sick."

Mr. March looked quite embarrassed.

Thomas felt miserable. It had taken over an hour to get him down. In the end Miss Peach had fetched a ladder, climbed up, and with a lot of gentle talking, which didn't come easy to her, she had managed to persuade a very shaky Thomas to make his way to the floor.

"Well," said Mr. March, clearing his throat, "Thomas jumped."

"Isn't he supposed to jump? Isn't that what they do in gym, jump?" said Mrs. Top.

"Yes," said Mr. March. "Not quite this *kind* of jumping, though."

"I'm sorry. You've lost me," said Mrs. Top, looking even more baffled.

The headmaster coughed. "Please sit down."

Mrs. Top perched on the edge of her chair
while the headmaster told her, using a lot of
pauses and ums, what had happened in the
school gym. He had to admit that it sounded
rather far-fetched.

When Mrs. Top had heard what the headmaster had to say, she stood up. "You have brought
me all the way to school because Thomas

jumped," she said. "I am sorry, but I don't understand what you are talking about, Mr. March. All I know is I should never have let him play games, after he'd been so sick."

"Thomas," said Mr. March, "will you please jump?"

Thomas looked at his mom.

"Do I have to?" he asked her.

"Yes, let's get this over with," said Mom wearily. "Then I can get back to work."

Thomas bent his knees and pretended to jump, keeping his feet fixed on the floor.

"There," said Mrs. Top. "There's nothing wrong with that. He's never been all that good at sports."

"Thomas," said the headmaster firmly. "I would like you to do a proper jump, not a pretend one."

Thomas looked from his mom's face to Mr. March and knew there was no way out. He closed his eyes and jumped.

He hit his head so hard on the ceiling that a chunk of plaster fell onto the carpet below. Thomas landed with a thud just as Mrs. Top fainted. She recovered to find the school nurse holding her hand and Mr. March pouring a cup of water. Mrs. Top felt flustered by all the attention and stood up, feeling weak.

"I think you should sit down until you get over the shock," said the nurse kindly.

"There is nothing to get over," said Mom, adjusting her coat. "We are just ordinary people and jumping very high doesn't run in the family."

"Quite so, Mrs. Top," said the headmaster. "All the same, perhaps Thomas should spend a few more days at home until he gets better."

There was no way Mrs. Top would be going back to work today. She took Thomas's hand and they left the school and walked home. She looked pale and worried.

"We won't have to tell Dad, will we?" said Thomas nervously.

"I am afraid we will," said Mrs. Top. "He would hear about it sooner or later."

Thomas knew this would be the worst part. His dad prided himself on having an ordinary family. They lived in a three-bedroom house that looked no different from any of the other three-bedroom houses on their street. Mr. Top had a regular job as a button salesman, and Mrs. Top worked in an office. They were ordinary people. Nothing extraordinary ever happened to them, and that was the way Mr. Top liked it. He would be none too pleased to hear that his son had done something as out of the ordinary as jumping as high as the ceiling.

That evening Mom told Dad what had happened at school. When Mom had finished, Thomas gave a demonstration.

His dad smiled and said, "Rita my dear, boys don't jump to the top of school gyms or hit their heads on kitchen ceilings. It is simply not possible for anybody to jump that high. I think this is a classic case of people letting their imaginations get the better of them." He laughed. "Perhaps, young man," he said, looking at Thomas's worried face, "April Fools' Day has come late this year?"

Thomas felt relieved. It wasn't exactly what he thought his dad would say. He had imagined he was going to be in big trouble.

"But Alan," said Mom, "you must have seen him jump just now. Thomas, do it again."

Thomas did as he was told.

"There, you see," said Mom. "That can't be normal."

"Rita, this is the last time I'll say it. Boys don't jump that high," said Dad, beginning to lose his temper. "I don't know what's come over you. You will be giving the boy all sorts of stupid ideas."

Thomas couldn't believe it. Surely his dad could see him jumping up to the ceiling?

"I think," said Dad sternly, "that Thomas just needs an early night. Then he will be as right as rain."

There was a terrible silence. Then Mom smiled weakly. There seemed little point in arguing.

"Perhaps you're right," she said. "It is all a bit strange."

"Of course I'm right," said Dad. "Now, we will hear no more about it. There's nothing wrong with Thomas. He is just an ordinary little boy. There's definitely no excuse for missing any more school. I will speak to Mr. March tomorrow and put an end to all this nonsense."

Thomas sat in bed that evening thinking about fairies. Fairies weren't fat, were they? All the fairies he had ever seen in fairy books were thin with beautiful long hair and wings that twinkled. They weren't fat and they didn't belch. It was hard to believe she was a real fairy, and even if she was, would she have the power to make a wish come true? But then, how did the fairy know what his real wish would be, or about Mom and the cupcakes? He lay in bed looking at the stars that shone bright in the night sky and thought about all that had happened that day.

Suddenly Thomas felt as if a lightbulb had gone on in his head. He finally remembered that he'd wished he could fly! He got out of bed and gingerly stood on his comforter. He wasn't quite sure what to do. Then he thought back to the gym. He seemed to go up when he waved his arms and legs. That's it, thought Thomas, that's what had stopped him from falling. This time he pretended he was swimming. He felt a little silly doing a hopeless sort of breaststroke in the air. Except it wasn't silly at all. He was way above the bed, flying around the room.

Thomas could feel the excitement from the tips of his toes to the top of his head. He felt it like a delicious feeling of melted chocolate. Thomas Top, nine years old: Thomas Top could fly.

6

The next day Mr. Top took Thomas into school and spoke to the headmaster while Thomas waited in the hallway. Mr. Top came out and so did Mr. March. "Glad we were able to sort out that little misunderstanding," said Mr. Top.

Mr. March also seemed relieved. "Now that I have had a night to sleep on it," he said, "I think you are right." He looked at Thomas. What were they all thinking of? Of course this boy couldn't jump that high. It was impossible! Really, this had all gotten out of hand. He was running a busy school, not a circus.

"We can safely put the whole incident down to an overactive imagination," said Mr. March.

"Exactly," said Dad.

That was the end of it, as far as the staff was concerned. His teacher, Miss Peach, who had never allowed herself the luxury of imagination, was only too delighted to agree with the headmaster. It must have been the stresses and strains of teaching that made them think that such an unremarkable boy as Thomas Top could jump that high. Thomas hadn't actually done anything extraordinary. He never had and he never would. He was just your average child. Nothing out of the ordinary.

Except his classmates didn't see it that way, and stories of Thomas's incredible jump quickly spread around the school.

At break that day, Neil, the biggest boy in school and a bully to boot, came over to Thomas and his friends.

"What you got in your shoes, Tommy Top?" demanded Neil.

"Nothing," said Thomas.

Shoes were a very sore point with Thomas. He would have loved to have had sneakers like everyone else in his class, but his dad insisted on him wearing sensible, ordinary brown lace-up shoes.

"Nothing," said Thomas again.

Neil didn't look convinced. "Well, that's not what I heard. I heard you jumped up and hit the ceiling of the school gym."

"Everyone just imagined that," said Thomas.

"I don't think so," said Neil. "Come on, you baby. Show us what you got."

Thomas paused. Since no grown-up believed he could jump that high, he had nothing to lose by showing the school bully that he could not only jump, but fly.

"Go on," said Neil, "bet you can't, Tommy Top. Bet you can't."

Thomas started doing his swimming strokes.

Neil burst out laughing and so did all the other kids who had gathered around to see what was going on.

"What are you . . ." laughed Neil, but he didn't finish what he was saying because Thomas was now flying upward. He was a little bit wobbly. It felt strange not having any walls or ceilings to stop him from going higher—and also a lot more scary.

"Miss Peach!" shouted a little girl. "Look, Thomas Top is flying!"

"It must be fun to have an imagination and be able to see things that aren't there," said Miss Peach dismissively.

Thomas was rather pleased when he came down and landed safely on the ground.

"Fantastic!" yelled Spud.

Neil, on the other hand, couldn't think of a single thing to say.

"I would shut your mouth before you swallow a fly," Thomas said to him, smiling.

A near riot had broken out on the playground. It took Miss Peach quite some time to get the children into class.

"Now settle down, children," said Miss Peach. "I don't want to hear any more stories about jumping or flying. Open your math books to page three."

After school finished, the whole class said they wanted to come to Thomas's birthday when he had it. This in itself was quite something. Usually nobody except Spud wanted to come to Thomas's parties because of Mr. Spoons, the magician, who did the same old magic tricks year after year. But Dad wouldn't hear of having anybody else. "We've had Mr. Spoons since you were five years old. It wouldn't be your party without him."

It was not surprising that no one ever wanted to come, especially when Suzi Morris had her party on or around the same day. Last year, she had had Aunt Hat and her Magic Handbag, and she had become the most popular girl in the school overnight. *Everyone* had wanted to go to Suzi's party. In the end she had only handed out invitations to those who had promised to bring the biggest and best presents. There had hardly been anyone at Thomas's party. But this year it was going to be different.

35

7

As the week went on, Thomas's flying got better and he became braver and bolder. He even had the nerve to fly over the school soccer field and get a ball that had been kicked high up in a tree. That had gone down well with his friends but unnoticed by Miss Peach. So far no grown-up had noticed him flying.

His most daring venture so far was to go to the corner shop and get some bread for Mom. Thomas had started walking. Then he wondered, as nobody was around, whether he could fly. It would be quicker and he could test if some people really didn't notice him while flying. There was only one woman out walking her dog and Thomas wondered if she would let out a scream when she saw him fly past. She didn't, but the dog barked wildly. Oh well, he thought, if no one can see me, then I might go a little bit higher.

He flew right up to the top of a building and sat there seeing the world in quite a different way, watching the sunlight play over the rooftops. No longer was he afraid of heights.

Then Thomas realized to his alarm that he wasn't alone. Sitting a little way off was a man in coveralls who was looking straight at him. Thomas felt a moment of panic. He only hoped that he was as invisible to this man as he seemed to be to everyone else.

"The Fat Fairy, I take it," said the man. Thomas stared, then nodded, hardly believing what he was hearing.

"How did you know?"

"Oh, I know all about the Fat Fairy. And I saw you flying around your garden the other day," said the man, with a huge smile on his face. "May I introduce myself? I am Mr. Vinnie, at your service."

"You can fly too?" asked Thomas in disbelief.

"How else do you think I got up here?"

replied Mr. Vinnie, laughing at Thomas's surprised face. "Why? Did you think you were the only person who could fly?"

Thomas shrugged. "I didn't think about it."

"What's your name, kid?" asked Mr. Vinnie kindly.

"Thomas Top," said Thomas.

"Nice to meet you," said Mr. Vinnie. "When I was a kid your age, the Fat Fairy gave me a birthday wish too, and like you, I wished that I could fly. I didn't know it at the time, but it was the best thing I could have ever wished for."

"It hasn't gone away, then?" said Thomas.

Mr. Vinnie laughed. "No, it hasn't gone away," he said. "I have been flying nearly all my life."

"I didn't think it would last," said Thomas. "I was wondering if one day I would just fall to the ground."

"Isn't that funny. I remember thinking exactly the same thing when I was your age. Then I met other boys and girls who could fly, and that was great. We grew up in the air, so to speak. We've all gone our different ways, but we still keep in touch."

"So there are others too," said Thomas. He found this to be a very comforting thought, though he couldn't quite think why.

"Yes, scattered all over the place," said Mr. Vinnie.

"And no one noticed you flying? Are you invisible like me?" asked Thomas.

Mr. Vinnie's face creased with laughter. "You are not invisible, Thomas. Neither am I, though I am more invisible than you because I am old and people don't take any notice of us old wrinklies at the best of times, let alone when we fly," said Mr. Vinnie. "No, Thomas, it's simple. Humans don't fly, so no one sees us." With that

Mr. Vinnie flew up into the air and turned a somersault before neatly landing on top of a pigeon, who did not like having his feathers ruffled by such a large bird.

"Wow," said Thomas. "How did you do that?"

"I've been at this a long time," said Mr. Vinnie. "Now show me what you can do, Thomas."

So Thomas did his swimming strokes.

Mr. Vinnie watched. "It looks exhausting. Don't you get tired?"

"Yes," said Thomas, "but I don't know what else to do."

"You don't need to wave anything around. You just have to trust that you can fly. A wish

41

is a wish, and it stays with you forever," said Mr. Vinnie.

Mr. Vinnie showed him how he could fly without moving his arms or legs. It looked so beautiful, as if he had control over the wind and the air.

Up on top of a building near the corner shop, while the sun was setting, Mr. Vinnie told Thomas all he knew about flying. Thomas flew home in great excitement.

Mom was very cross. "Where have you been and what have you been doing and where is the bread?" she said.

"I'm sorry. I forgot it," said Thomas. He hadn't meant to. It was just the thrill of flying and meeting Mr. Vinnie. It was no use saying all that to his mom. She wouldn't understand.

"Oh," she sighed, "head in the clouds, I suppose."

"Yes, I suppose," said Thomas with a small smile.

8

At first, the magic of flying was so wonderful that it hadn't really mattered that no grown-ups were aware of what an incredible thing Thomas could do. In fact it had been very useful. It had given him a freedom without which learning to fly would have been impossible. But as he got better, he began to feel more and more sad that his mom couldn't see what he could do. His dad had said nothing, even when he had sat in the garden watching Thomas do somersaults in the air. It felt disappointing that neither his mom nor dad could see just how good he was.

As the evenings got lighter Mr. Vinnie and Thomas would meet in the park, where they could fly properly without buildings getting in the way.

Mr. Vinnie said that it was sad that so many people walked with their heads bowed down, looking out for dog poo, and not seeing the magic that was all around them. The more Thomas flew, the more he thought how wonderful everything was. Being so high up with the birds made you see the world in a very different way.

Mr. Vinnie told Thomas about his dad and how when he was young he had wanted him to get a proper job, like being a banker. "But once you have flown up where the sky is blue,"

said Mr. Vinnie, "you couldn't be tied down to a desk and imprisoned in four walls." So he had become a painter and decorator, which was just the ticket. He could work faster than anyone else in the business. Flying up and down meant there was no need for ladders and he could float on his back to paint ceilings.

Thomas found that he could talk to Mr. Vinnie in a way that he had never been able to talk to his dad.

"Do you have any kids?" Thomas asked Mr. Vinnie as they sat one evening at the top of Alexandra Palace, watching the sun setting over London, turning it from red to gold.

"No," said Mr. Vinnie sadly. "Annie, my dear wife, and I wanted kids but that didn't happen." Mr. Vinnie smiled. "I am not complaining. Annie and I had a wonderful life together." He had often taken his wife flying. She couldn't fly, but Mr. Vinnie was a strong man and, as he told Thomas, his wife was as light as a sparrow. Sadly, she had died last year and Mr. Vinnie said he thought at the time that he would never fly again. But then one day he had seen Thomas flying in his garden and he felt that he couldn't give up, not when there was so much magic in the world.

"I'm sorry," said Thomas.

"No need, Thomas, but thank you," said Mr. Vinnie. "Annie would have loved to have met you."

It is hard to imagine your parents being young, and when Thomas thought about his dad, he couldn't see him as a kid laughing and enjoying himself. Dad was more interested in Thomas doing well in math and things like that.

"There's no money to be made in having fun," said Dad. "To get a proper job you need math." Math, Dad told him, is the cornerstone of your future. But Thomas was no good at math, whereas flying was something he could do perfectly. Dad, thought Thomas gloomily, could suck all the fun out of a day without even trying. It was like their dreaded fishing trips.

Fishing was Dad's one little hobby. He bought every magazine and book on the subject. He prided himself on having the latest fishing rod and the most up-to-date equipment. There was

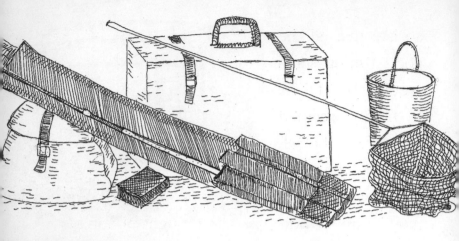

nothing Dad didn't know about fishing except how to actually catch a fish.

He would pack the car very carefully on Saturday morning, bright and early, making sure nothing was left out. It took forever, and if Dad couldn't find this or that, they would have to stop everything until it was found. By the time they set off, the day was no longer bright, because Mom and Dad would have had a long argument.

The reservoir was a dreary place that backed up onto the local gasworks. This was where Dad liked to go fishing, but they would arrive

so late that all the
good fishing spots
would be taken.
It hardly seemed
worth all the ef-
fort. In the end,
there wasn't that
much time left to
catch a fish. They

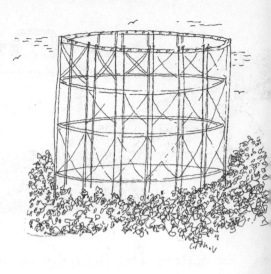

would both come home tired and frustrated
and Thomas would wait for the awful words:
"We'll get it right next time, son." His dad always
said it and they never did.

There was no doubt that Dad worked hard.
Except for Saturday fishing trips, he would
spend the weekends studying his button sale
numbers. Mom would sit alone at the kitchen

table looking through magazines and dreaming of what her house would look like if only she could paint it the way she wanted. Dad had painted it magnolia and brown when they first moved in. Nothing out of the ordinary—and that was the way he liked it.

A sadness now seemed to hang in the air like a mist. It had definitely gotten worse since Thomas had taken up flying. Dad had become more rigid, seeing less and less of what was around him. At times Thomas felt sorry that the Fat Fairy had been unable to give him his original wish, that his dad could have fun. Then maybe everything would have been all right.

10

School was much better than it had ever been before. Thomas had gone from being unnoticed, with only one friend, Spud, to being one of the most popular boys in school. This was in no small measure helped by the fact that teachers couldn't or wouldn't see what Thomas could do. It gave him an edge over all the grown-ups, and a feeling of power, which also frightened him a little.

His friends, like Spud, found it hard to believe that Miss Peach, who had seen Thomas jump and hit the beams in the gym, could not now see him fly. It seemed unfair to Thomas that his teachers would get cross with him for acting as though he were playing soccer with four left feet and never seeing that he was amazing, a star. In the air, Thomas had a beauty and a grace that gravity had never given him. All he

wanted was for just one grown-up to say, "Look, there's Thomas Top flying!"

Then one Thursday, not a very remarkable day, he had flown as usual at recess doing a round of the playground and a few spectacular twists before going in with the others. Then he had sat in a very dreary lesson, daydreaming. He was interrupted by Miss Peach shouting at him.

"Thomas Top, are you listening? You are to go and see the headmaster immediately!" She

was reading a note that had been handed to her by the school secretary.

"Why?" asked Thomas.

Miss Peach looked very red and blotchy. "Thomas, just do what you are told, and take your coat and backpack with you," she said angrily.

This wasn't a good sign.

Sitting in the headmaster's office was his mom. She had been crying. Thomas felt he must have done something really wrong, but he didn't know what.

"I'm sorry, Mrs. Top," Mr. March was saying, "I don't know exactly what Thomas is doing, but whatever it is, it is making all the children over-excited. We can't cater for a child who is disruptive."

Thomas couldn't believe what he was hearing.

"I therefore think a suspension is the only course of action open to us, and we can review the case after the school board has had their meeting."

Mrs. Top said nothing, just took Thomas's hand and they walked home in complete silence. Thomas knew his dad would not be pleased. He would be grounded for weeks—maybe years. His party would be canceled, he thought miserably, and that would be a shame, especially when there were so many people coming.

"It's not fair, Mom," said Thomas when they got home. "I didn't do anything wrong. I just flew around the playground and got balls out of trees. That kind of thing. I wasn't bad or anything like that. And everybody liked it, and they all want to come to my party, and now I won't be able to have it."

Mom sat at the kitchen table, her head in her hands.

"Mom," said Thomas, "all I want is for someone to see that I can fly and that I'm not making it up. I haven't been disruptive, whatever that means."

Mom looked out the window at the birds flying past and said almost in a whisper, "I know,

Thomas. I've seen you out there flying, and in my heart I am so proud of you. But what could I say when your dad and all your teachers refused to see it?"

Thomas put his arms around his mom's neck. "I'm sorry. I didn't mean to upset you."

"Oh, I know you didn't. It's not your fault, Thomas. What I would give to have wings like you and be able to fly!" said Mom.

"I don't have wings," said Thomas.

"I know," said Mom, "and you're right. You can do something so wonderful and magical that it fills me with envy. What is it like up there?"

"Pretty good. Really good, actually. People don't notice you. Only children and dogs stare. I have even flown up High Street with my friend Mr. Vinnie," said Thomas proudly.

"Who is Mr. Vinnie?" said Mom.

"He's a painter and decorator who can fly like me. There are a lot like us, Mr. Vinnie says, but I have only met him. There's not so many kids now because they don't wish for it very often anymore."

"Why not?" said Mom.

"They wish for things like beauty and brains and long hair and to be the best computer whiz in the world. It's getting rare, Mr. Vinnie says, for kids to wish for simple things like flying," said Thomas.

"I see," said Mom, who was seeing Thomas with new eyes. This was her son, her little baby, this incredible boy who knew all about flying! "Well, I think we should invite Mr. Vinnie around for dessert. I would very much like to meet him," said Mom, smiling. "Would you like to call him and see if he can come next Tuesday?"

"But what about Dad?" said Thomas.

"I'll talk to him," Mom said.

11

That night there was a terrible argument in the house. Thomas had never seen his dad so angry. He wouldn't hear a word Mom had to say. "Are you crazy, Rita?" he shouted. "Boys don't fly!"

Thomas's party was canceled.

Dad phoned Mr. Spoons, who said he was sorry to hear it, but pleased to know that boys these days still got punished for being bad.

"He hasn't been bad," said Mom desperately. "He has only been flying."

"Will you put a sock in it once and for all with all this flying nonsense!" yelled Dad, going blue in the face. "We are an ordinary family. Flying is for fairy tales."

"I can't take much more of this, Alan," cried Mom.

Thomas went to bed with tears running
down his face. He could hear Mom
and Dad in the kitchen shouting
at each other, even when he pulled his pillow
over his head.

The next morning things were not much
better. Dad didn't say a word during breakfast
and left for work still not speaking. Mom had

to call the office where she worked to say she wouldn't be coming in for a week, or until she could get some child care sorted out. "I'm going to lose that job if I have to take any more time off," she said to the kitchen wall.

"I'm sorry," said Thomas, who had just come in and was standing behind her, tears pricking his eyes. Mom turned and smiled.

"It's not your fault. Come on, don't look so sad," she said. "It's just hard being grown-up. Sometimes we fail to see the magic in the world, and that's our problem, not yours."

Things didn't get any better over the weekend. Although it was sunny outside it felt like winter in the house. Dad was only speaking in yeses and nos. He went fishing by himself after making a huge fuss about a fishing hat that he couldn't find.

Mom had let Thomas have Spud over to play while Dad was out. They spent their time behind the back of the garden shed.

"What's in there?" Spud asked.

"I don't know. Dad doesn't let me go in. He

says it's just for the lawnmower," said Thomas, kicking a stone.

The boys talked about Thomas's party and how bad it was that it had been canceled, especially when it had been the most talked-about party in school for ages.

"Well," said Thomas, "in a way I'm glad it's not happening. Can you see everybody sitting there and watching Mr. Spoons's magic show for babies?"

"You would have to do a lot of flying to make up for that," said Spud.

On one thing they both agreed: The school was wrong for suspending Thomas just for being good at flying.

"It's not on the school curriculum," said Spud. "Too bad."

"Hey, wouldn't it be great if Miss Peach had to give flying lessons?" said Thomas.

"I think," said Spud, "the teachers at our school are the living dead."

Thomas laughed. It felt good to be outside with your best friend and the sun shining. Thomas soared up in the air and down again, Spud running after him. It looked as if Spud was chasing a kite shaped like a boy. On the last run around the garden, Spud hit the door of the garden shed by mistake and to his surprise it burst open. Thomas landed next to him

and they pushed the door open a little farther.

"We shouldn't go in," said Thomas. "Dad would explode if he found we'd been snooping."

"There's something behind the lawnmower," said Spud.

Thomas looked again, his eyes getting used to the gloom of the shed. Spud was right. Whatever it was, it was hidden well, with a large tarp covering it.

"Go on," said Spud. "I'll keep a lookout."

Thomas hesitated in the doorway. But his curiosity got the better of him and he squeezed in carefully so as not to disturb anything. He lifted the cover gingerly and looked underneath.

What Thomas was expecting he didn't really know, but he was amazed at what he saw: a beautiful old motorcycle with a sidecar, its chrome shining like stardust. It looked almost new. The boys stood looking at it openmouthed.

"Do you think your dad stole it?" asked Spud.

"No," said Thomas, "Dad would never do anything like that."

Still, he had to agree with Spud that it was a

bit weird for Dad to have such a great motorcycle hidden in the garden shed. They quickly put the cover back and made sure the door was properly locked this time.

Mom brought them out some lemonade and cookies, saying Spud should probably go home soon. The boys sat eating on the grass.

"A mystery," said Spud. "Maybe your dad has another life that you don't know about."

Thomas didn't think so. He couldn't see his dad ever having that much fun.

12

It seemed to take forever for Tuesday to come around. Why is it, wondered Thomas, that the things you look forward to seem to take so long, and then when they finally come, they seem to go so fast? But at last Mr. Vinnie arrived, looking very stylish. He was wearing an old flying jacket.

Mom had put dessert out in the garden on a table laid with a white linen tablecloth and a bunch of flowers. Thomas had helped her make a cake. He had great fun putting in the strawberry jam and whipped cream.

Mom and Mr. Vinnie got along really well, and she asked him all the questions that Thomas thought a non-flying grown-up might ask. Like, Is it safe? Will Thomas hurt himself? Could the wind carry him away? Should he only go flying

when it's sunny? Mr. Vinnie ate the cake, which he said was delicious, and assured Mom that Thomas was doing very well and there was no need to worry.

"Would you like to see what flying is like, Rita?" said Mr. Vinnie.

"You mean fly up there? It's not possible," said Mom, blushing.

"Oh yes it is, Mom, it is. Tell her, Mr. Vinnie," said Thomas in great excitement.

Mr. Vinnie told her about Annie, his wife who was a non-flyer like herself, and how they had flown together.

"You used to fly to France, didn't you?" said Thomas, who now couldn't wait to show his mom what it was like.

Mom stood in the middle of the garden. Mr. Vinnie took one hand and Thomas held the other.

"What do I do now?" said Mom, feeling rather foolish.

"Nothing at all, just hold on to us and don't let go."

No sooner had Mr. Vinnie said this than Mom realized she was way up above the ground, looking down on the little gardens and houses that lay like a patchwork quilt beneath her.

"Oh, this is wonderful!" she cried. "Oh, this is magic!"

13

"What do you think you're doing, Rita?" shouted Dad as Mom landed back in the garden.

"Flying," said Mom proudly.

"And who is this man? What is he doing here?" said Dad. He did not look at all happy. Mom tried to explain and so did Thomas and Mr. Vinnie. Dad was having none of it.

"I've had enough of this madness. What has come over you, Rita?"

It had ended very badly. Dad had shouted at Mr. Vinnie, saying he had no right to come here invited or not, and he was going to hold Mr. Vinnie personally responsible for all this flying nonsense. Thomas was sent to bed early, and once again he could hear his parents arguing downstairs.

70

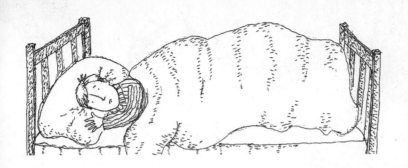

The next morning he found Mom sitting alone at the kitchen table. Her face had a sad upside-down look to it. Dad had already left for work.

"Why is Dad so angry?" Thomas asked her as he was eating a bowl of Wheetos. Mom looked out of the window and up at the pale blue sky.

"I think it's Dad's work that makes him so unhappy. He is probably a bit like you, bullied at work by his boss for not getting the right amount of button sales."

"I'm not bullied anymore," said Thomas.

"I know," said Mom. "It doesn't work, being ordinary. Being ordinary is harder for some than being extraordinary."

"I think you're right," said Thomas.

Mom made a cup of tea and told Thomas what his dad had been like when she had first met him. He was so different from the other young men she knew, and that was what she loved about him. He *was* out of the ordinary. Like his motorcycle, which had a sidecar and a name like a movie star—Harley-Davidson.

"What happened to the motorcycle, Mom?" asked Thomas. He didn't want to tell her he'd seen it.

"Oh, it's in the garden shed," said Mom. "But do you know, Thomas, your dad used to be a whiz at magic tricks? He could make flowers come out of his hat and coins from behind his ears."

"What happened?" said Thomas. "Why isn't he like that now?"

"Dad wanted so much for you. He was going to make us a fortune. We were all going to live in a grand house. Dad was going to be king of the button sales. Except it didn't quite work out that way," said Mom sadly. "He thought he had to be grown-up and responsible, and he just got stuck. Time that goes so slowly for you just flew by for us. We lost our dreams. Anyway, Dad thought dreams were for kids."

Thomas thought, Well, that explains the mystery of the motorcycle. How weird, he thought, to own such a wonderful machine and keep it hidden in the garden shed. It was not all his dad had kept hidden, Thomas thought miserably.

Thomas knew it was bad. His mom had gone to stay with her sister and she wasn't back. Today was Saturday, his dad's birthday, and he should have been having his party. He lay in bed wondering what was going to happen. He had made Dad a card and a little present, a painted box for his fishhooks. He was about to get out of bed and give it to him when the front doorbell rang and he heard a familiar voice. He got out of bed and ran downstairs in his robe, forgetting his slippers. His dad was standing in the doorway.

"I don't know what you want," he was saying. In front of him stood the Fat Fairy.

"It's quite simple, Mr. Top. You are Alan Top, Thomas's dad?" said the Fat Fairy.

"Yes," said Dad.

"I am here to give you a wish."

"Is this some kind of practical joke?" said Dad. "Because if it is, I am not in the mood."

"No," said the Fat Fairy.

"Dad," said Thomas, pulling at his sleeve.

"Thomas, not now," his dad said sharply. "Can't you see I have some ridiculous salesperson selling something or other?"

"I am not selling anything," said the Fat Fairy. "Do you want this wish or not? I am not standing here all day waiting. I have other places to go, other wishes to give."

"What do you mean, a wish?" said Dad.

"Oh dear. It is quite simple. You wish for something. When you've wished for it, I give it to you and I can be on my way," said the Fat Fairy, folding her arms firmly.

"I don't understand," said Dad. "Which company are you from? They should know better than to let you go walking around the streets looking like that, your wings all lopsided and your tiara looking like it's been sat on."

"Oh give me strength," said the Fat Fairy. "Have you any notion what I've been through to get here? It's amazing you were given these two wishes. Never known it to happen before in one household."

"Please, Dad, just wish," said Thomas.

"You were here for Thomas's birthday," said Dad, looking puzzled.

"Yes, I gave your son a wish. Now I am back to give you one," said the Fat Fairy.

"I don't need it," said Dad.

"Please, Dad," said Thomas again. He could see the Fat Fairy was on the point of leaving.

"Sorry, I can't hang around, dear," she said.

"Please, please Dad," said Thomas, who now felt quite desperate. "Wish to have fun."

"That's quite enough of this nonsense," said Dad. "Just pull yourself together, young man."

The Fat Fairy turned and started to walk away.

"You've ruined it," said Thomas angrily, "like you ruin everything." He was going back inside when he heard his dad say almost in a whisper, "I wish I could have . . . fun."

It was too late. The Fat Fairy was too far away to hear. Dad was still standing with the door open when suddenly the Fat Fairy turned around and looked at Dad. She gave a loud belch and said, "All this wishing plays havoc with my insides," and with that she was gone.

15

Dad closed the front door and started saying "You see, nothing has changed." Then he looked at Thomas as if he had never seen him before and started to laugh and laugh and laugh. Thomas looked at him, worried at first that something had gone really wrong. Then he realized that Dad wasn't laughing a hollow, shallow laugh, but a laugh that comes when you are enjoying yourself.

"Oh Thomas, oh Thomas, did you see what I saw? The fattest fairy in the world. Well, it's made my day. Don't think I've laughed like that in ages."

"Yes, Dad," said Thomas, "it's your birthday treat. Happy birthday!" He gave his dad a big hug.

"What did I do," said Dad, still smiling, "to have such a boy as you?"

Thomas went upstairs to get his card and present for Dad, and Dad went into the kitchen to make breakfast for them both. When he came down Dad was standing there looking at the wall.

"Awfully dull this room is. I never noticed it before," he said.

"Yes," said Thomas. "Mom wanted to paint it full of color."

"I stopped her," Dad said sadly. "What an idiot I've been. Is it too late?"

"No, Dad," said Thomas. He went over to the drawer where Mom kept her scrapbook full of all the paint samples and colors she would like to paint the house. Dad looked at it.

"We'll do it. We will paint it for her just like she wants," said Dad. "Oh no, we can't! We wouldn't be able to do it in time. She would come back and find ladders all over the place and—"

"Dad," said Thomas, "my friend Mr. Vinnie is a painter and decorator."

"I don't know about that. I think I was pretty rude to Mr. Vinnie," said Dad.

"It doesn't matter," said Thomas. "If I tell him that the Fat Fairy came, he will understand."

"Why would he understand?" said Dad.

"Because he was granted a wish when he was my age, and he wished to fly," said Thomas.

"Like you. All this time you've flown and like a fool I've pretended not to see. Life is just too dull and ordinary for that kind of magic. But now it's as if a mist has risen. My eyes have sparkles in them."

They had breakfast together. Thomas gave Dad his card and the little box he had painted,

which Dad said was the best box he had ever had. After breakfast, they called Mr. Vinnie, who came around right away. In no time at all Dad, Mr. Vinnie, and Thomas had gotten one room painted. With two flying painters and Dad doing the baseboards, it didn't take long.

Dad and Thomas had one of the best days they had ever had together. In the evening they ate take-out, sitting on the kitchen floor, laughing and telling jokes.

Mr. Vinnie asked Dad if he remembered any of his magic tricks. Dad did and said he had a few of them still locked in the garden shed. It was just beginning to get dark when they went out, and there along with the box of magic tricks was the covered motorcycle. Thomas felt a little guilty because he knew what it was.

"What's that, Dad?" he said, pointing to the tarp. Dad pulled the cover off and there stood the Harley with its sidecar gleaming in the darkness.

"Well, I never," said Mr. Vinnie. "What a beauty!"

Dad smiled the broadest smile Thomas had ever seen.

"I used to take Rita out on it. We had a good time together. When Thomas was little, we took him as well. We went to the seaside, we went all over the place . . ." He stopped. "I'd forgotten all the fun we used to have."

"It doesn't matter," said Mr. Vinnie. "Why don't we see in the morning if this old thing works?"

"You could go and pick up Mom," said Thomas excitedly.

"Then me and my young flying helper will help finish the painting," said Mr. Vinnie.

16

The next morning bright and early, Mr. Vinnie turned up with a freshly baked loaf of bread, which they ate in large slices with melted butter. It tasted like white clouds. They filled the motorcycle with gas and to everyone's amazement it worked right away.

Mr. Vinnie loaned Dad his flying jacket and goggles. He looked great riding off on the motorcycle, and it made the most wonderful putt-putting noise too.

Thomas and Mr. Vinnie worked fast. They finished the living room and Mom and Dad's bedroom. They laid the table the way Mom

liked it, with a white tablecloth and a bunch of flowers from the garden. Mr. Vinnie and Thomas felt very pleased with themselves.

By the time Mom came back the whole house shone and smelled of new paint. Mom cried with joy.

"Oh my word! What have you done?"

Dad came in with Mom's suitcase.

"Do you like it?" he said.

Mom turned to look at him. "This was your idea?" she said, amazed.

"Yes, I've been a fool, Rita. For too many years I've wanted to be like everybody else. I never saw what an extraordinary family I have. Being like everybody else means you don't exist. I didn't leave it too late?" he asked anxiously.

"No Alan, you haven't left it too late. But what's happened to you?" said Mom.

"Well, I think maybe it's your birthday present," said Dad.

Thomas looked a little baffled. As far as he knew Mom had not given Dad a birthday present.

"The Fat Fairy you sent me," said Dad. "She made me laugh so much."

Mom looked at Thomas and at Mr. Vinnie and smiled. "What did you wish for?" she said.

"I wished to have fun," said Dad sheepishly.

"Oh Alan! Oh Alan Top, I love you!" said Mom.

17

Dad was quite a different person after that. On Monday he and Mom went to see Mr. March, the headmaster, who agreed to take Thomas back as long as he kept the flying down. It didn't matter as much to Thomas that some people still refused to see what an amazing thing he could do. The most important people in his life knew, and that was all that mattered.

Dad rearranged Thomas's party and they didn't invite Mr. Spoons. "He's good with babies but not for you, son," said Dad. Instead Mr. Vinnie came over to help Thomas give his friends a flying tour around the garden. Mom made a wonderful lunch and Dad did some truly amazing magic tricks. It couldn't have been a greater success. When everybody had gone home Thomas stood in the garden with Dad, looking at the sun setting.

"Next time Mr. Vinnie comes around we're going to take you up there," said Thomas. Dad laughed. "Then I'll have to cut down on the ice cream," he said, giving Thomas a hug. "Go on with you. I know you want to be off up there, but don't be too long."

"Thanks, Dad," said Thomas.

18

Thomas flew to the park and sat at the top of Alexandra Palace. It was his favorite place up here with the birds. He was thinking about how wonderful it was to fly when out of the blue the Fat Fairy landed next to him.

"Hello, Thomas," said the Fat Fairy.

Thomas couldn't believe his luck. "How great to see you again," he said.

"Just popped by to see how you're doing," said the Fat Fairy. "I've been watching this story unfold, dear. It tickled my fancy."

"Do you know all my friends are looking for you?" said Thomas.

"Everybody's looking for me, dear, but they don't often find me," said the Fat Fairy, smiling.

"I want to thank you for making it all all right," said Thomas.

"No need. I liked the wish you made about your dad having fun. It touched me, it really did," said the Fat Fairy. "But you can't wish for other people."

"Do you choose who to give wishes to?" asked Thomas.

"No, that's not in my power. It's the Chief Fairy's decision and he's an old grouch. Always grumbling, and he doesn't have to do the legwork."

Thomas laughed.

"You should see him. Beats me why he should complain so much. He sleeps most of the time. All he has to do is give me a list of people and off I go. Out in all kinds of weather, I am."

"Do you always go back and check on people?" said Thomas.

"Occasionally I have to go and remind someone what they wished for," said the Fat Fairy.

"Why?" said Thomas.

"Well, gone and forgotten, haven't they," said the Fat Fairy.

Thomas found it hard to believe anyone could forget a wish given by her.

"People grow up and they forget all sorts of things. Like your dad. It had gotten so bad with him that he had to wish for fun before it could happen."

"It was the best wish ever," said Thomas.

"I thought it would be," said the Fat Fairy.

Thomas looked at her lopsided wings and her tiara glinting in the evening sun, and said, just to make quite sure Mr. Vinnie was right, "My wish won't leave me, will it?"

"Oh, bless your cotton socks. No dear, once you've wished for something, you've got it for life, whether you like it or not. That's why, Thomas, you've got to be careful what you wish for."

"I'm very happy with my wish, and so is Dad with his," said Thomas.

"You both should be. You wished for sensible things, things that could happen. Well, I can't sit here all day chatting to you. Must be on my way. But before I go, I have one more wish for you," said the Fat Fairy.

"What's that?" said Thomas.

"I wish you all the best, Thomas Top."